# SPACE MAC

*Emma Jane*

Cocky escort Mackenzie "Mac" Jones has just the right type of blood so that when he steals an odd silver brooch from a client, it transports him to a strange planet. Frightened and confused—and confronted by aliens—he flees and ends up bumping into a handsome humanoid male named Teevar.

But Teevar and his companions are also on the run, and Mac finds himself embroiled in the affairs of his new friends with no idea how to get back to Earth. Can Mac and Teevar survive long enough to work out their feelings for each other? And will Mac ever see home again?

A NineStar Press Publication

Published by NineStar Press
P.O. Box 91792,
Albuquerque, New Mexico, 87199 USA.
www.ninestarpress.com

Space Mac



ISBN: 978-1-947904-37-8

Printed in the USA
First Edition
December, 2017

Also available in eBook

ISBN: 978-1-947904-36-1

"You understand us now? Yes?"

"I don't think he does. You made the chip too strong. Look at his eyes! I don't think they're meant to be that red."

"The chip is fine. His eyes are probably meant to do that." Then to Mac, "Can you understand us?"

Mac stared. He had an odd metallic taste in his mouth, but it disappeared when he swallowed. He frowned at the men as they peered at him.

"What the hell did you do to me?"

"Translator chip; you didn't have one."

"Very primitive," said the other man. "Backwards even. Are you sure he has the right make-up?"

"He wouldn't have activated the pin if his blood was incorrect. I'd say his species is a cousin of some sort. Look at him. He looks almost kovan."

Now that the men had released him and stood back, discussing him, Mac raised a hand and touched the back of his head. He couldn't feel a hole, and when he looked at his fingers, there was no blood.

"Take a sample quickly. Then we'd better put him back."

Mac blinked at the men. "What the bloody hell is going on?" he asked. "Who the fuck are you guys?"

One of the men crouched in front of him and gave him a smile as if he was a simpleton. "What species are you?" he said, slowly.

"What...what?"

"Species." The men exchanged a look and one rolled his eyes.

Mac glowered at them. "This is all very funny," he said. "I'm a *human.* You guys are dickheads. Now, if you don't mind, I'm going to get the fuck out of this...whatever the hell this situation is, and leave. Martin will be paying me double for this. Bloody weirdo. I'm going to have to add more clauses to my profile now, you know that?"

"Human." The men looked at each other again.

"Never heard of it," one said.

"Does it matter? Just make a record of it. Human male. DNA match. Get the cell sample."

"This is, like, role play, right?" Mac asked. "Just drop the act now. One of you can get my bloody clothes for me, and then I'm off. Tell Martin to shove it up his arse."

As he stood to leave, one of the men moved suddenly and pushed something hard against Mac's thigh and clicked the end of it, sending a searing hot pain into his flesh.

"Jesus Christ." Mac doubled over and clasped a hand against the wound as the man removed the device. He could only lower himself back into the chair, his skin burning with indignation. He blinked and tentatively removed his hand. Again, there was no blood, but an angry red welt blemished his perfect skin.

"What *was* that thing? You people can't keep sticking things in me. I feel violated." He looked for the...whatever it was, but the men had secreted it away. "Right. I'm leaving, right now! I'm going to have you people blacklisted! Tell Martin nobody's going to fuck him now."

He got up, but one of the men reached for him saying, "We will send you back."

Mac twisted out of the guy's grasp, shoved the other man out of the way, and ran for the door. They shouted after him, but it only spurred him on. He reached the door, pulled it open, and emerged into another room that *still* didn't look like his client's house. White walls again, but this was a laboratory of some sort, and Mac was buggered if he was going to hang around and let the weirdos perform sex experiments on him. They came after him, so he ran on, out of that room and into a corridor of yet more white. Cursing, he chose a direction and sprinted onwards, his bare feet slapping the floor.

The air crackled and voices sounded out. "*Attention. Subject loose. One human male. Not dangerous. Not intelligent. Needs apprehending. Will respond to Ethan Smith. Michael Harris. James Johnson. Mackenzie Jones. Aidan Peters...*"

Mac almost stopped. How the hell did they know all his aliases? And they knew his real name. Not intelligent? Bastards! They were probably some big-city escort agency looking to put him out of work or recruit him. They'd probably been watching him. Well, he wasn't standing for any of that bullshit!

Footsteps echoed down the corridor behind him, and he bolted to the nearest door and pulled it open.

Light dazzled him. Noise hit him, and when he could see again, he gaped at the sight before him. The ground beneath his feet was dusty sand, the buildings all around him were a mishmash of styles and from different eras—tall, glass-fronted office buildings, wooden shacks straight from a Western, oddly shaped bricked cottages, glass domes... Vehicles buzzed in the sky like something out of a science fiction novel.

Someone yelled, "Out the way!" and Mac pressed himself back against the door as a man rode past on a creature that looked like a short-eared giant rabbit.

"What the actual fuck?" Mac didn't have time to take in anything else. Voices from behind the door alerted him they were still coming after him, so he ran across the street and disappeared into an alley between two of the giant office blocks. He kept running, changing direction, twisting and turning, and doubling back until he was certain nobody would find him.

Then he stopped, sank down to his backside, and wondered if Martin had drugged the juice.

THE SAND, WHILE not unpleasant beneath his feet, was working its way up his arse-crack and reminding him he was still naked. If he was tripping, or...whatever the hell was happening...then he could at least not be naked about it. He stumbled down the alleyway, distractedly wiping sand from his skin, and kept an eye out for anything he could use to cover himself with. The buildings seemed to come straight out of the ground on either side of him, no doors or windows, the walls made from glass he couldn't see through. Mac stopped and eyed his reflection, running a hand through his hair to tidy it and peering at his bloodshot eyes.

*A dream*, he thought. *I'm in a dream*. He couldn't remember whether he was ever aware he was dreaming when he dreamt, but he was aware of it now. He pinched the skin on his arm, but the sensation didn't wake him.

Sighing, he turned to look back the way he had come. Nobody came after him. No Kevins or whatever the hell they called themselves.

"Martin?"

He waited but nobody replied to him. He didn't know if talking in a dream meant he would be talking in his sleep. Nobody had ever told him he talked in his sleep—none of his clients, none of his partners. A girlfriend once told him he snored, but he'd been a smoker at the time, and since he'd given up, he'd had no comments on the matter.

The alleyway ended at a street, or a sort of street. It was an open, dusty area, opposite which there were more buildings, and along which people walked and chattered and rode weird rabbit-beasts.

Mac laughed a little. "No more cheese before bed," he muttered. Nakedness in dreams was supposed to mean something, but Mac was buggered if he could remember what. Something about shame and embarrassment, probably. He felt neither and never had done about nudity. He looked great naked. He stood, hands on hips, watching the scene before him with a strange sense of detachment.

"Hey! Hey, you!"

Mac turned towards the voice. A man, dressed in red to match his red face, ran at him. Mac raised his hands to warn the guy off, but the man tackled him to the ground, turned him onto his front, and dragged his arms behind his back.

"Ow, bloody hell!" Mac protested. "Careful!" Something cold clasped his wrists, and he realised he'd been cuffed.

"You are under arrest for indecency in a public place," the man said. "You will be taken immediately—"

"I'm dreaming," Mac explained, as he was hauled to his feet. "Everything's okay."

"—to the holding cells at Baska Hall and kept until judgement is brought upon you. You do not have to say anything—"

Mac frowned as the man took off his red coat and covered him. "Hey, do I get a lawyer in this dream, or...?"

"You will be assigned a lawyer. And maybe a doctor to assess your mental health."

"Great, yeah, I need one of those."

Mac allowed the man to pull him along the street. He was aware of people watching him. He was also aware, when he looked closer, that some of the people didn't look quite human. There was a face with more eyes than he could count at a glance, blinking out at him from a slender frame draped in black. A creature resembling a giant insect or a walking twig strode past him, its arms and legs long and gangly. Women—two of them—gazed at him from across the street, but when he looked again, a film passed across their eyes and they licked their lips with forked tongues.

The man stopped pulling him along as they reached a large silver sphere; he waved a hand and a door opened up before him.

"In you get," he told Mac.

"What...?" He didn't really know how to finish his sentence, so he didn't bother. Dazedly, he staggered into the sphere, and the man followed. There was nothing inside but two chairs, and Mac sat because he didn't know what else to do and his head was beginning to spin.

The man sat beside Mac and performed a few more hand movements. A brief vibration passed through the sphere before both chairs rose into the air and floated in the centre. Mac cursed. Two belts snaked from the seat, one across his lap and the other across his chest, and held him secure. He swallowed hard and chanced a look at the man to see if he looked like he knew what he was doing.

Then, the sphere disappeared, or seemed to. The inside became transparent. With the outside world visible once more, they moved forwards—the man controlling their direction with subtle flicks of his hand.

Mac laughed at the madness of it all and then, as buildings whizzed by faster and faster, he threw up and passed out.

# Chapter Two

DUST TICKLED HIS nostrils. He sneezed and woke himself up. Mac took a moment to realise he lay on his side in the dirt, that he was not in Martin's bed, and that usually when you woke up from a dream you actually left the bloody thing. He scrabbled upright, heart pounding, and retreated to the back of the cage—cage, he was in a fucking cage!

*Not a dream.*

He was naked, again, the red coat gone. But his hands were free and there was fabric on the ground before him that he snatched up and, once he'd worked out where the arm holes were, put on. It was a white, scratchy, trouser-and-top number that made him feel like a criminal.

"I am *not* made for burlap!" he yelled, hoping someone somewhere was listening to him. "My skin will not take this shit!"

He hugged his arms around his waist and approached the front of the cage. Metal bars on three sides of him; cold stone wall at the back. The sky above was blue, and the sun beat down as if he was in the Sahara. He knew now though that he wasn't even on Earth anymore. Aliens walked past the cages—he was in a row of them, most occupied—and nobody paid him a blind bit of attention.

A bang on the bars to his left made him jump out of his skin, and reluctantly, he looked over.

"You look kovan," the creature said. "But you smell like an oosh dog from one of my planet's moons. Possibly Steplar—the oosh dogs are particularly rancid on Steplar."

Mac gazed at her. It *was* female. She had the body of a woman—light blue fabric draped over all the right curves—but her face was more angular, and she had two great, curved horns coming from her head like those of a ram.

"And you look like a goat," he told her. "A particularly old goat, who's all haggard and not even good for a curry."

She grinned at him and leaned against the bars. "I like you, oosh dog. What are you here for?"

Mac scratched the back of his head and moved a bit closer. "To be honest, I'm not really sure. I don't even know what's going on or where I am."

"Ah, you have been at the tonic? Your frame is small. You should drink less."

"No, I'm not... I'm not *drunk*. There was this...thing, this pin..." He stopped and stared wide-eyed at the ground. The pin. He'd dropped the fucking pin! It was probably his key to getting home. For fuck's sake.

"I see. I am Lenara." She reached with her hand through the bars, her forefinger extended towards him. He wasn't entirely sure what the gesture meant, but he had the feeling he'd offend her if he ignored it. Mac took hold of her finger and shook it.

"Mackenzie Jones," he said, too befuddled to think up a lie. "Human, by the way."

Lenara withdrew her hand and eyed her finger with a bemused smile on her face.

"Human," she repeated. "I've not heard of your species, I am sorry."

"Don't worry about it. I don't know what you are either. I don't know what any of these...people...are. I'm...my planet hasn't ever really done space travel before. You know. Not to anywhere other than, like, Mars or something. Do you know Mars?"

Lenara shook her head, the horns making the movement slow and heavy. "No. My species, the veneks, are from a planet called Nevka. I do not think any of us have heard of Mars."

"Nevka. Huh. I thought it'd be Venekasia or Veneksta or something. Although, I guess it'd make more sense if humans were from Humania." Mac frowned to himself. Then he shook his head and looked at Lenara. "I'm from Earth."

"Do not know it."

"No." Mac sighed. "Look. So, I'm in a heap of shit here, and I have no idea what to do or how to get myself out of it—"

"You want out?"

Mac frowned. The way Lenara said it made him instantly suspicious, as if she were about to do something incredibly dodgy or reckless or dangerous. Or all three.

"Yeah," he said. "I can't stay here."

"Good." She flashed her teeth at him—like human teeth but wider, flatter. "Then we get out. Little human, you watch and be ready."

He didn't really know why she called him 'little,' as they were pretty much the same height. She was a touch taller, perhaps, and muscled, but he sure as hell didn't feel little in comparison. He watched as she moved to the front of her cage, plucked something from between her breasts, and threw it out into the crowd.

For a moment, nothing happened. Then came a *clack clack* call, like that of a magpie, shortly followed by another from across the way. A large animal sprung up from the crowd and flapped its great wings before descending on whatever it was Lenara had thrown. The other creature, which had echoed the first call, also leapt into the air and launched itself in an attack against the first. They reminded Mac of lizards with wings.

*Dinosaurs*, he thought, watching as they scrapped over the object, flapping and cawing and biting and clawing. People moved quickly aside, shouting and screaming.

Two guards—or police officers, since they wore the same red uniform as the man who'd arrested Mac—jumped into action, calling for order and waving batons.

Mac, distracted by the commotion, had momentarily forgotten about Lenara until the cages shook. When he looked, she lowered her head and rammed the bars between their two cages again and again until the metal buckled and bent, and she squeezed herself into Mac's space. Before he could say or do anything, she turned and butted the front of his cage until the bars warped enough for her to squeeze herself through. She reached for his hand and pulled him after her.

"Run now," she told him. "Follow me."

Prisoners shouted after them—some spurring them on, some demanding they free them too—but Mac dashed after Lenara, aware now that the guards had spotted them and were in pursuit. He was pleased the ground was soft beneath his bare feet as he struggled to keep up with her fast pace and she twisted and turned and pushed her way through the people.

"Hurry," she snapped, stopping only briefly to snatch his hand and pull him onwards.

"We're gonna get caught, and we're gonna die." Mac managed to gasp the words out between breaths. Lenara didn't seem to care. Or listen. She pulled him down an alleyway, out into another open area full of trading stalls and onwards still until they reached a space filled with aircraft. *Spacecraft.*

Mac stopped when Lenara did. He huffed and panted, his hands on his knees and a stitch in his guts. "Not...run like that...for a while," he said. "Don't really...do the gym anymore."

Lenara clicked her teeth at him and waved a hand in a gesture he took to mean shut up. She scanned the ships until she spotted one she seemed to recognise, then, looking back over her shoulder, she took Mac's hand again and tugged him after her. He was too knackered—and scared—to protest, and so he followed her up a ramp into a small green ship and simply coughed when the doors closed behind him.

Everything was dark.

"They won't find us here," Lenara said. "This is my ship. *Veena*. Are you okay, human? You sound like death."

"I'm okay. Call me Mac, please. Human sounds weird." He straightened and realised he could see little spots of light in the room. "Are we alone?"

"No."

Lights came on, causing Mac to screw his eyes shut until the pain passed and he could open them again. He was in what he presumed was some sort of cargo bay or loading area—an open space filled with crates, with a staircase at the back leading up into the rest of the ship.

A human-looking man, a kovan he guessed, descended the staircase and approached him and Lenara. Mac blinked. The man was pretty good-looking, with short close-cropped blond hair and striking blue eyes. He wore a simple beige tunic, brown trousers, and fabric shoes. A gold emblem of some sort hung from a chain around his neck. He raised an eyebrow at Mac before addressing Lenara.

"I've been waiting a while. Where have you been?"

"Ran into trouble," she explained, moving past Mac. "It's okay. No bother now; do not worry yourself."

"Don't worry myself? You don't seem to have any money on you. That's the whole reason we came here. What were you doing down there?"

Lenara waved a hand.

"She got arrested," Mac explained. "We both did. Then we escaped. Mackenzie Jones."

Mac held out his hand for the man to shake, but instead he eyed Mac's hand as if he didn't know what to make of it before he tentatively touched his forefinger to Mac's.

"Teevar Nok Dimar."

"That's your name, right?"

"We don't *need* money," Lenara said. "We have him." She jerked her thumb back at Mac. "He is *human*. Have you ever heard of such a thing? We sell him." She continued on her way up the stairs, leaving Mac gaping after her.

"Nobody's selling me!" he called. "Hey! I am not for sale!"

Teevar sighed. "I am a *priest*, Lenara. Selling people is highly against everything—"

"Priest," Lenara scoffed. She stopped at the top of the stairs and clicked her teeth. "Some priest." She turned away from them both, opened a door, and disappeared from view.

Mac looked at Teevar. "I need to get off this ship and get my pin back."

Teevar's brow creased as if he couldn't understand what Mac had said. He made a vague noise and waved a hand, dismissing Mac, before hurrying after Lenara.

"Wait!" Mac called. "Bloody hell." He turned to the door and tried to work out how the damn thing opened when the whole ship *juddered*. He reached out to steady himself and realised suddenly, his blood running cold, that they were taking off.

"No! Shit, balls, bollocks, and bloody bastards." Mac turned and ran up the stairs after Lenara and Teevar. "Don't you bastards dare take off! You hear me? Wait!"

He yanked open the door they had both gone through and emerged into a corridor. More doors were along the walls on either side of him, and he dragged a hand through his hair, eyes wide.

*Piss*, he thought.

He was about to choose a door at random and hope for the best when the one closest to him opened and Teevar appeared.

"I am sorry. Gods forgive me." He reached for Mac's face. Mac's instinct told him to move away, but something sharp pricked his skin before he could, and the world spun around him.

"Arsehole," he muttered. And then he fell back.


MAC DREAMT HIS teeth were falling out. The feel of them, like stones in his mouth, made him spit blood and enamel. He woke with a start and clenched his jaw, relaxing when his teeth met in his mouth. He sighed, rubbed his face, and then frowned at the ceiling.

The room was made of metal. He sat abruptly. It appeared he was in bed at least, but the walls were cold and hard and far too *cell*-like for him to feel comfortable. He got to his feet, tugging at the rough itchy clothes he still wore.

So, he'd been beamed up to another world, had been assaulted, arrested, run from the police, and now was soon to be sold into slavery. As shit experiences went, it had to be pretty near the top.

The door to his room opened, and Teevar entered carrying a tray of food.

"You can't treat me like this," Mac growled at him.

"I'm sorry. Sit, please."

Mac sat on the bed. His stomach rumbled and he realised he was actually quite interested in whatever Teevar had for him. Unless it was poisoned. Or toxic.

Teevar sat beside him and placed the tray between them. "Protein and vegetables," he explained. "I wasn't sure what your species ate. Water too." He pointed at a cup of clear liquid, and after a moment of Mac staring at him suspiciously, he added, "All safe to eat."

"I guess as you want to sell me, you're not looking to kill me," Mac said, picking up a brown cube and eyeing it.

"I will try to talk Lenara out of that, I promise. There might be another way; we could always keep running."

Mac popped the cube into his mouth and chewed. It didn't taste unlike beef, so he helped himself to another piece. "What are you running from?"

Teevar shook his head and studied his hands in his lap—delicate hands, Mac noticed, soft. "Bounty hunters," he said quietly.

Mac raised his eyebrows. "So you're criminals. And what, you think you can pay the bounty hunters off, right? That's why you need money?"

"Yes."

"What did you do?" Mac shovelled more food in his mouth, laughing a little when he discovered one of the vegetables tasted exactly like Brussels sprouts.

"Nothing."

"Bullshit."

Teevar stood. "I'm sorry you've been involved in all this. Enjoy your meal."

"Wait." Mac jumped up and grabbed Teevar's arm before he reached the door. Their gazes met, and Mac let go. "This is all *so* fucking weird for me. I just want to go home."

"Do you have people waiting for you? Family?"

*Nobody*, Mac thought. As a child he'd been in and out of foster care—he had no idea what had happened to his birth parents, or whether he had siblings or not. All his most recent relationships had been for money, and his friends...well, they were fair-weather friends, disappearing whenever things got tough.

"A wife," he said. "Two kids. They'll be worried about me. They won't be able to feed themselves without me to provide for them. I *need* to get home; you need to help me."

Teevar gazed at him, the conflicting emotions clear on his handsome face. "Where is your planet?"

"Earth," Mac said. "I have no idea."

Teevar grasped Mac's hands and held them tight. "If we find Uff, we will take you home."

Mac had the biggest urge to pull Teevar even closer and kiss him. Instead he pulled his hands gently free and said, "Earth."

"Earth." Teevar smiled a little. "My apologies." He cleared his throat and stepped back. "I will bring you some better clothes. You're a similar size to me so..."

"Something that doesn't chafe," Mac said. "And maybe something fitted, so it shows me off a bit. I've got a great body."

Teevar's cheeks flushed red, and he nodded before quickly making his getaway. Mac grinned and turned back to the bed to finish the rest of the food. Maybe he could just get Teevar and Lenara to fly him home, and then he wouldn't need to go back to that scary building and find his pin. He wondered what Martin thought—he'd probably discovered it missing and Mac—*Ethan*—gone and thought the worst.

Mac shrugged, not particularly bothered. Hopefully when Teevar came back, he'd let him know where he could get a shower too. His feet were black, and he felt sticky and dirty beneath his clothes.

When he'd finished eating and Teevar still hadn't returned, he went to the door and opened it to peer into the corridor. Pleased that they hadn't locked him in, he wandered out and decided to investigate. The ship was pretty much how he imagined spaceships to be, except maybe less shiny and not as futuristic. Actually, it looked more like something from Earth and not at all like an alien spaceship. He opened doors to sleeping quarters, a kitchen, an engine room, and a large empty room, which, when he entered, he saw had a glass roof looking out to the stars.

Mac stood in the centre of the room, gazing upwards. His soul soared. The universe was *fucking* beautiful.

"Lovely, isn't it?"

He turned at Teevar's voice. The man had a bundle of clothes in his arms, and he raised them to show Mac before joining him in the middle of the room.

"Thanks. Hey, is there anywhere I can wash?" Mac took the clothes, raising his eyebrows in appreciation of the softness of the fabric.

"Back in your room," Teevar said. "The other door leads to a washroom."

Mac nodded.

They stood in silence. Mac turned his attention back to the stars before Teevar cleared his throat. "There's nobody following us. We're quite safe."

"Did you speak to Lenara about the whole not selling me thing?"

"Yes. She can see no other options at the moment."

"Not even the keep running option? If there's nobody following us then everything's okay, right? We can go find Earth."

Teevar smiled a little. "They always find us eventually, even in the great expanse of the universe."

"Bloody hell." Mac had to hope they either changed their minds or he could find a way to get himself out of trouble before anybody appeared who they could sell him to. "Is it just you two here?" he asked.

"Myself and Lenara, yes."

"And you're what, friends?"

"I suppose so. When I fled from my planet, I needed a ship. Lenara had a ship—she was on the run too; we sort of fell in together."

"That planet we just left—that wasn't your home world?"

Teevar shook his head. "No. My species is part of the population, but it isn't where we originate."

"What's Lenara running from?"

"On Nevka, females have power over males. Lenara fought for equality—she's an anarchist. She caused a lot of trouble for her people."

Mac folded his arms. "I'm male and she wants to sell me. So much for equality."

"I think she'd sell you if you were female, too."

"Well that's bloody marvellous then." Mac pushed past Teevar and headed to the door. "I'm going to wash and change and try to get my head in some sort of order."

He stomped out, ignoring Teevar calling him back, and made his way back to the room he'd woken up in. He put the clothes on the bed and then opened the door to the washroom. The room was slick and empty, with no sink or shower or bath or even any taps. He stepped inside and the door closed softly behind him.

"Weird," he muttered. He felt along the walls for a hidden button but could find nothing. If he looked up at the ceiling, he could make out holes where he presumed water came out. "How the hell am I meant to have a wash in—"

Warm water rained down on him, making him gasp and curse. He quickly pulled his clothes off and dumped them on the floor, not caring that they got soaked. He let the water run over his body and wash away the dirt and stress.

Once he'd finished—and it turned out the room had a blow-dry function too—he went back into his room and picked an outfit from the clothes Teevar had given him. Nothing was quite *him*, being modest and mostly brown, but it fit and was quality material. After he'd changed, he sat on the bed and thought about what to do, idly scratching the patch on his thigh where the kovans had done whatever it was they'd done to him.

He really had *no* options, he realised, other than hope that Teevar could convince Lenara to change her mind, and that they would keep running and eventually run into Earth. He'd probably end up famous— the space traveller who'd brought aliens to Earth. It'd probably make him rich too. Actually, it was starting to sound pretty good.

He lay back and thought about Teevar. The man was a priest, but he'd done something criminal. Mac couldn't see that he would have murdered anybody—he seemed too soft and shy and, well, religious. He'd probably broken some sort of religious law like eaten meat or mixed his fabrics or something. Mac closed his eyes, and eventually, he drifted off to sleep.

# Chapter Three

WHEN MAC WOKE, it was dark in his room. He sat up and rubbed his eyes. "Who turned off the lights?"

The lights came on, and he blinked. "Lights," he said again, and the room plunged into darkness. He laughed.

"Lights."

This time when the lights came on, he stood up and stretched. He'd go speak to Lenara himself, he decided, and convince her that selling him was a very, very bad idea. He straightened his clothes, fussed with his hair, found some shoes, and headed to the door. God, his teeth felt fuzzy—he ran his tongue over them as he walked, deciding to ask Teevar about toothpaste and toothbrushes the next time he saw him.

He wondered if it was night-time. Then he attempted to work out how to tell if it was night-time in space, and then he wondered who was flying the ship, if it was indeed night-time, and consoled himself with the probability that Lenara and Teevar either took it in shifts or there was an autopilot.

Spying a staircase, he headed towards it and climbed up, his feet tapping ever so softly. At the top, there was another door. He opened it, trying to be as quiet as possible, though he needn't have worried.

Lenara sat in the cockpit, her back to him. Lights flashed on her console and the view from the window in front of her showed nothing but black. She turned briefly when he entered, but didn't speak.

"Are you busy?" Mac asked before he shook his head. "Actually, I don't care if you are busy. I need to talk to you. You can't just go around kidnapping people and selling them—that's against their human rights...alien rights..." He waved his hand in frustration. "Whatever, you can't do it. I'll run as soon as I get chance, you know."

Lenara chuckled. "Where will you run to?"

"Well..." Mac flapped a hand at the window. "Space. I'll get a suit and float away or flag down a passing ship. Or I'll scarper as soon as we land. I'll kill myself! I'll kill myself, and then what will you do?"

Lenara turned to him. "Do you have any talents? If you are worth more to us than the price we could get for you, there is no point in selling you."

"I have many talents," Mac said. "I'm excellent in bed, I make the *best* scrambled eggs, and I can juggle. How much are these bounty hunters after to leave you alone?"

Lenara sighed. "Probably more than you are worth." She turned back to her console and touched one of the screens. "See the map? We will reach this little moon soon; there is a commerce station there. We have goods in the cargo bay that we can sell. If we get a good price..." She shrugged.

"Right. Great! Hey, I'm bloody good at haggling. And bullshit. I bet I could get you an excellent price. What is it you're selling?"

"Jiks," Lenara answered. "Nuts."

"Nuts." Mac screwed up his nose, pretty certain nobody in their right mind would want to pay much for nuts—and from the way Lenara said it, he could tell they weren't worth much. "You mean, like, edible nuts, right?"

"Edible nuts," Lenara confirmed.

"Well...let me sell them for you. Just have Teevar explain to me about how the whole currency thing works with you people, and I'll get you a good deal on that moon. Then you can do me a favour and not sell me."

Lenara looked at him from the corner of her eye, and then she smiled. "I knew I liked you, little human. We have a deal. You have roughly four hours to learn. Go."

Mac almost threw a salute, realised that'd look silly, and instead nodded and left the cockpit. It actually felt *good* to be doing something.

MAC FOUND TEEVAR in the room with the stars. The man was sitting cross-legged in the middle of the room with his eyes closed and incense burning all around him. Not wanting to intrude in case he was praying, Mac hovered near the door, fiddling with the cuffs on his jacket and wishing they were a little slimmer.

"Mackenzie?" Teevar opened his eyes. They shone a bright and beautiful blue.

"Mac's fine." He moved into the room. "We need to talk. I have a plan." He flashed Teevar a grin and then rattled off everything he thought he'd need to know before making a deal with people on the moon. Teevar listened quietly before answering all his questions—probably giving him more information than he needed. When they finished talking, Mac was sitting opposite Teevar, playing with one of the burners.

Teevar reached over and stilled Mac's hand. Their gaze met.

"Are you very religious?" Mac asked.

"I'm a priest." Teevar moved his hand away and folded it with his other in his lap.

"You probably wouldn't be a big fan of mine back on Earth," Mac said. "Or you might be. It depends what you worship, I guess. Pagans were big into sex and drinking and all that. You might worship your god with your body for all I know."

The fact that Teevar's face had gone very red told him otherwise.

"Gods," Teevar said. "There are five of them; one to watch over each season. I worship them through prayer and my actions—I meditate—I hope one day to join with them on the higher plane."

Mac leaned back, resting on his hands, and gazed up at the stars above. "I'm not religious. I fuck everything with a pulse—and I get paid for it—I drink; I used to smoke. I don't pray, and I curse like a sailor. But all this—" He waved a hand at the stars. "—makes me think there might be something else out there after all. A god, I mean, looking down on Earth. I think I'll pretty much believe anything now."

He lay back after a moment, and Teevar got up and joined him, laying down at his side.

Mac turned his head and gazed at him. "You look so human."

Teevar smiled and met his gaze. "And you look so kovan."

Mac opened his mouth to tell Teevar what the other kovans had mentioned—that their species must be related—but then he wondered if that'd lead to questioning and him having to say what they'd done to him. Why had they done that to him? He frowned and looked at the stars instead.

THEY LANDED ON the moon among hundreds of other spacecraft. Lenara pulled the crates behind them on a trolley, while Mac and Teevar wandered ahead, with Mac trying to take everything in with wide eyes. The moon bustled with activity, and all kinds of alien life forms were on show—words Mac couldn't understand, that his translator chip couldn't fathom, reached his ears, and he twisted his neck to catch a glimpse of who was speaking. He spotted insect-like creatures with mandibles clicking and clacking and quickly looked away when their gazes met.

"This place is mad," he whispered to Teevar. "Like nothing I could've imagined."

The surface of the moon was grey and dusty and little clouds of the stuff poofed up into the air as they walked. The place had gravity and an atmosphere, but when Mac looked to the sky, he could see the vastness of space. Teevar had told him there was a generator somewhere that controlled the atmosphere and allowed them to walk around without spacesuits on—it was easier to do business with somebody who wasn't wearing a spacesuit, after all.

He wondered where they would meet their potential buyers and hoped he could do as he'd promised and blag himself a good deal. The spacecrafts towered over them—they were all different shapes and sizes. Mac couldn't see any flying saucers, though he did look. They stopped near one that looked like a small, black fighter aircraft, and Lenara let go of the trolley.

"We wait here," she said.

Mac could smell spices and smoke and food. He grinned at Teevar, excited despite everything.

Teevar smiled back at him. "If we make enough, we could buy you some better clothes."

"I'm going to make enough to be able to go on one hell of a shopping spree, don't you worry about that." He rubbed his hands together in anticipation. Food, he'd buy food too—he was pretty confident he could smell bread somewhere, and his stomach growled.

"They come." Lenara peered down the way they'd just walked.

"These are the guys who love these nuts, right?" Mac asked Teevar. "This is gonna be easy."

Three large, reptilian-like men—Mac guessed they were male—strode towards them. They were heavily muscled, and Mac noticed each one had a gun at his hip. As they drew closer, Mac noticed their faces were shorter than a reptiles and that they lacked a tail, though tight, snake-like scales covered their skin.

"Jiks," one said, spotting their crates. "I smell jiks."

"Jiks," another agreed, nodding his head.

Mac stepped out in front of them, and opened his arms wide. He plastered a smile on his face. "Jiks indeed, gentlemen, and only the finest available. In fact, these are grown in the fields of Kentassa and ripened under the three suns. Would you like a taste?"

The lizard men—skreens, the name Teevar had told him came into his head suddenly—moved closer to the crates, their tongues flicking at their lips and their eyes hungry.

"Wait, I have some already opened." Mac reached into his pocket and took out a parcel, which he quickly unwrapped to reveal a handful of pale-coloured nuts. "Here."

Each skreen took a nut and popped it into his mouth with surprising delicacy. When they swallowed, they looked to Mac for another, and he offered them out until his hand was empty.

"They're good, right?" he asked. "The best."

"It's okay," one said. "They will do."

Mac laughed. "Okay? My friend, you will not taste better." He sighed. "But, if you only think they are okay, then I think we should take them elsewhere—I would hate for you to buy something you didn't enjoy." He waved a hand at Lenara for her to take the crates away and, frowning at him, she picked up the trolley handle to do just that.

"A moment." One of the skreens moved to stop Lenara and tapped the crate instead. "We talk prices."

"Six thousand boules. An absolute bargain, gents. I'm sure you'll agree. That's two a crate, plus one free. You can't say fairer than that." Mac caught the look Teevar gave him—he'd told him the crates were worth four thousand, maximum, but Mac ignored him and instead opened up one of the crates. "Just look at the quality of them. No nasty wormy holes in these jiks."

The skreens looked at one another before one lifted his chin at Mac. "Four thousand."

"Four thousand will buy you two crates, and to be honest, gents, I'm a bit offended. No freebies for that offer."

One of the skreens growled, and one shook his head and made to turn away. Lenara slapped Mac's arm in annoyance.

"Five, that's the best I can do," Mac said. "And you're robbing me at that price."

"Five. We have a deal." The skreen turned back and extended his forefinger. Mac touched it with his own finger and turned to flash Lenara a brief triumphant grin.

"A pleasure doing business with you," he said. He watched as Teevar took fabric bags from the skreens and checked the boules inside.

"All in order," Teevar confirmed, stepping back so the skreens could take the crates. "Thank you."

Mac watched, feeling very pleased with himself as the skreens took the trolley and headed away.

"Now can I go shopping?" he asked.

"Make it quick," Lenara said. "It won't be long before they realise two of those crates were filled only with empty shells."

Mac's mouth hung open as Lenara wandered off and engaged with a seller nearby. Then he laughed. "Shit. Did you know about that?"

Teevar blushed. "I'm afraid so. Come on, we really must be quick now."

"You people are dodgier than I am, you know that?" Mac slapped Teevar on the back as they wandered between the ships together, looking at what was on offer. "So, clothes and food. Lots of clothes and food, and maybe one of those gun things the skreen guys had."

"I suppose you've earned it," Teevar said.

"Too bloody right."

It wasn't long before Mac's nose led him to the food, and he chose what he wanted and let Teevar handle the money while he went off and found himself several new outfits, and a shiny new pistol that, when he was allowed to test it, fired off bolts of light.

They had just turned back to find Lenara and make their way back to the *Veena,* when Teevar stopped abruptly and tugged Mac's arm to get his attention. Mac followed Teevar's gaze and noticed a cage beside one of the ships with some sort of dog creature inside, muzzled and shackled.

"What's that?" Mac asked. The creature wore clothes, so he presumed it was more than an animal. It looked feral, though, and bloody dangerous. Its body was lithe and sinewy; it had a tail like a monkey's and eyes like a wolf's.

"A lupa," Teevar said. "They come from the same planet as the skreens. Wait here."

Before Mac could protest, Teevar was off and haggling with the vendors. Mac saw boules change hands and then, tentatively, the cage was opened and the lupa dragged towards Teevar. Mac held his breath as Teevar released its shackles and removed the muzzle.

*He's gonna get eaten*, he thought. *Crazy, handsome devil.*

Then the lupa turned and was gone, running through the crowd and away without as much as a thank you. Teevar joined Mac once again.

"We should go," he said.

"And what was all that about? You're suddenly against slavery now? Or is it a guilt thing?"

Teevar didn't have time to reply. There was a shout, and Lenara came jogging towards them.

"Back to the ship, quickly," she said. "The skreens know."

"Oh, shi—" Mac ran when he spotted the skreens rounding one of the spaceships—their weapons drawn and murderous looks on their faces. He ran with Teevar and Lenara back towards the *Veena*, ducking and cursing when shots rang out around him.

He spied the *Veena* ahead, but a quick look back over his shoulder told him the skreens were gaining on them. Lenara had already reached the ship, being quicker than both he and Teevar, and she opened it and disappeared inside, yelling at them to hurry.

Mac took out his weapon and fired a warning shot when Teevar tripped and fell. He shoved his gun back into its holster and pulled Teevar up.

"Come on, they're nearly on us!"

"Can't run," Teevar gasped.

Mac dragged him on anyway. A shot whizzed past his ear, and then pain exploded through his right arm. He cried out and looked at the bloodied wound ripped into his skin. Nausea washed over him. Teevar said something to him, but he didn't catch the words. He thought he'd black out.

Then the skreens cried out in surprise and diverted their fire elsewhere. When Mac looked back he saw the lupa had returned and had launched itself at one of the skreens—it clung to its back with its teeth sunk into his shoulder.

The next thing Mac knew, Lenara reached out to him and pulled him up the gangway into the ship, with Teevar by his side. They all turned together just as the lupa leapt free from the melee and raced to join them. Lenara slapped a control pad on the wall and the door closed just as the lupa made it inside.

Mac's heart pounded so hard he thought his chest might burst open. Lenara abandoned them all to start the engines, and Teevar peered at Mac's arm in concern. The lupa grinned at them with pointed teeth.

"That felt *good*." The voice sounded female.

Mac blinked at her. "I've been shot. I've been..."

Teevar took his arm gently. "Let's get that looked at. Come on."

Mac let Teevar take him to a room he hadn't seen yet, which he presumed was the medical bay judging by how sterile everything looked. He sat down on the bed in the middle of the room before he fell down. Teevar rolled up Mac's sleeve and eyed the wound.

"A graze," he said. "You were lucky. I'll clean it up for you."

Mac didn't feel particularly lucky. He was too light-headed to argue though, so he watched as the lupa came and leaned against the door frame as if she was watching a show.

"I am Ral," she said.

"That's nice," Mac muttered.

"Teevar Nok Dimar," Teevar said, as he bustled around Mac. "This is Mackenzie Jones. Our friend the venek is Lenara. Thank you for your help with the skreens."

Mac could only sit and frown to himself as Ral shrugged. He winced and cursed as Teevar cleaned his wound.

"We were very fortunate to find Ral," Teevar said, as he dabbed a cotton-like pad into some pink liquid and wiped it over Mac's arm again. "The lupa have a bite that is venomous to the skreens."

"That bloody hurts," Mac growled.

"We were fortunate to find each other," Ral said. "You help me, I help you. We're even." She came into the room lifted her chin at Mac. "Your blood doesn't smell like the blood of a kovan."

"That's not my problem," Mac replied.

"He's human," Teevar said. Then to Mac, "This might hurt a little." He positioned a metal pen-like instrument over Mac's arm and a laser fired out, sealing the wound.

Mac yelled out and gripped the edge of the bed so hard his knuckles turned white. When Teevar finished, he jumped up and backed off, inspecting the wound in his shoulder—now no more than a scar.

"Sorry," Teevar said.

"I've had enough of today." Mac stalked to the door. "I'll be in my room. And don't go disturbing me, as I'll be trying on my new clothes." He glared at Teevar and Ral, and then turned and left.

*Bloody pain in the arse aliens.* He collected his clothes from where he'd dropped them down in the cargo bay by the door and then returned to his room.

He vaguely wondered if the skreens would come after them now that they'd ripped them off and set a lupa on them. Then he decided he didn't bloody care anymore, and if they came after them, he'd shoot the whole damn lot of them. He laid his clothes out on the bed and admired them. They certainly felt better quality than anything he'd ever seen on Earth, but he had no idea if they were more expensive. What was the boule to pound conversion rate?

He busied himself with trying on his clothes and then styling his hair and preening himself. When he grew bored with that, he picked up his gun and admired it. It was made of a sleek, black metal, and Mac realised it looked more like a sex toy than a gun.

*Will I ever have sex again?* He'd have to find himself a sexy alien, and it'd have to be kovan if he wanted it to look human. He didn't fancy Lenara or Ral's species much. He thought about Teevar. Had the man been so forward-thinking that he'd paid for Ral's release in the hope that she'd help them when the skreens caught up with them? Maybe. Teevar seemed quite smart.

He holstered his weapon and lay back on the bed. Could Lenara find Earth? Would she bother looking? He'd done his bit. He supposed they'd have to find the bounty hunters now and pay them off. That'd probably go wrong too. Well, as long as he wasn't shot again.

He stifled a yawn with his hand, and closed his eyes.

MAC WOKE TO the sound of somebody tapping on his door. He yawned, fussed with his hair, and then got up to see who was bothering him.

Teevar looked him up and down, his cheeks colouring red. "You've changed."

"I said I was trying on my new clothes. I know I look great; you can pull your tongue in."

Teevar gave him a puzzled frown. "Pull my...?"

"Never mind. What did you want?"

"Lenara thinks we're safe. The skreens aren't coming after us and there's no sign of any bounty hunters. No other ships around at all, in fact."

"Right. Good."

Teevar touched Mac's arm. "Are you still in pain?"

"No." He shrugged Teevar's hand away, even though the touch stirred something within him. "You could've told me about the nuts, you know. What if they'd looked in the wrong crate? And what was all that about with Ral? You freed her, yet you would've gone ahead and sold me."

"Nobody's selling you."

"Too bloody right they're not." Mac scowled at Teevar, but he realised he didn't feel as angry as he probably should've. He sighed. "Do you want to get something to eat?"

"I came here to ask if you wanted to join us," Teevar said. "Lenara's cooked up quite the feast."

Mac followed Teevar out and along the corridor. "Who's flying this thing while she was cooking?"

"We're stationary." Teevar smiled at Mac and then opened the door and gestured for him to enter the room.

Lenara and Ral were already seated at the table, though Lenara stood when they entered. Mac's eyes widened at the food on offer, and his stomach growled. Although things *looked* strange—odd-shaped fruits and meat that was slightly greyer than he would've liked—it all smelled completely normal. He sat himself next to Ral and reached for something he thought was bread, though it had an odd, squishy texture when he touched it.

He began eating, pausing when he noticed Teevar had his head bowed in prayer, his hands clasped around the golden emblem he wore, but nobody else stopped so he carried on. By his side, Ral crunched through bones just as if she were a dog.

"This is weird," Mac said. "It smells like lavender, looks like bread, but feels like a sponge. Doesn't taste half bad though. Kinda like naan."

"I have no idea what any of those things are," Teevar said. "But I'm glad you're enjoying it."

They ate in companionable silence for a little while until, the food dwindling, they made conversation.

"Tell me your stories," Ral said between licking juices from her fingers. "How does a venek, a kovan, and a hooman end up being chased by the skreens?"

Mac raised his hands. "No idea. I was beamed here. I've just been trying to stay alive since."

Teevar cleared his throat. "I'm sure your story is far more interesting, Ral. Perhaps you should tell us how you ended up a slave."

Ral shrugged. She pushed a bone around on her plate and then picked it up. "I was drugged. I woke up where you found me. Some...*people*... they see a lupa and they think 'there is a good pet, or a good soldier,' and they take." She bared her teeth. "That is how the skreens show us to others; they don't like that *we're* the superior species. If we were more numerous, we could wipe them out."

Teevar reached across the table to touch Mac's hand to get his attention before withdrawing. "A hundred years ago, the kovans and the skreens were at war—some dispute over ownership of a moon—and the lupa were our allies. We won the war, and to reward our friends, we gave them stewardship of the moon. The skreens, they—"

"They blew up the moon," Ral said. "Killing thousands of my species."

"But that was a hundred years ago," Lenara added. "And now there is peace. Of a sort. There are no weapons now that could destroy a moon."

Mac looked from Lenara to Ral and then to Teevar.

"On my planet," he said, "there was a great war between the Martians and the Plutonians. I mean, those guys were batshit insane with their killing of everything. The Martians won. Then they took all our spaceships and buggered off back to their own planet, Mars, and the Plutonians, well, they had their planet demoted. It's just a big moon now or something. Anyway, they're all pissed off about it and don't visit Earth anymore, not that it was our fault. We were innocent bystanders in it all."

"Politics," Teevar said, sighing.

"Yeah." Mac took a handful of red berries he'd liked the taste of and popped them into his mouth. "So, what's the plan now? We find out how to get to Earth, right? I'll take you guys there. You'll love it. I'm really important there too, so you'll be rewarded for bringing me back."

"How important?" Lenara asked, a suspicious frown on her face.

"Very important," Mac said. "People worship me. I think it's my good looks. You take me there and not only will you be rewarded, but we'll keep you safe from the bounty hunters too—and the people who set the bounty."

"I know a man named Kelrar D'aminar who is the finest mapmaker in the solar system," Lenara said. "If he has no map to Earth, then it doesn't exist."

"Right, and he's easy to find, is he?" Mac asked.

Lenara smiled. "For me, yes. He is...an old friend of mine." She got up from the table, inclined her head, and then set off to the cockpit.

Mac looked at Teevar. "You'll like Earth," he said. "You'll fit right in."

# Chapter Four

MAC DIDN'T KNOW where they were going, and it seemed to take far too long to get there. He occupied himself by sitting with Lenara in the cockpit—declining her offer of a piloting lesson—and then watching Ral exercise in the star room.

"I can teach you how to fight," she said, flashing her sharp teeth at him.

Mac folded his arms. "How do you know I don't already know how to fight?"

"No muscles," Ral said. "No coordination. And when you fired at the skreens, you missed."

"I only missed because I'd never fired a weapon like that before," Mac protested. He uncrossed his arms and stood before Ral as she raised her palms to him. "What do I do then?"

"Hit me."

Mac wasn't convinced he'd do a very good job, but he felt like he was representing the entire human race and didn't want to look like a wally, so he raised his fists. Imagining he was Bruce Lee or Jackie Chan, Mac swung a punch at Ral's palm, going for speed and accuracy. She twisted aside and used her hands to guide him past so his momentum made him stumble forwards.

Ral laughed.

"Hey, that's not funny! You weren't supposed to move."

"You tell your enemy that the next time you go to shoot them."

"All right. Show me your moves then."

Mac sparred with Ral, picking up a few tricks and inventing some moves of his own, until he collapsed back on the floor, laughing. He hadn't realised somebody was watching them until, over by the door, Teevar cleared his throat. Mac sat up.

"Impressive," Teevar said.

Mac scratched the back of his head, a little embarrassed. "Me or Ral?"

Teevar smiled at him, making him certain of the answer, but as he came into the room, he said, "Both of you. I just came to tell you both we're about to enter the planet's atmosphere. We'll soon be there."

Seeing as he had the most invested in this trip, Mac left the room to join Lenara in the cockpit. He sat by her side and watched as she piloted the spacecraft. "This Kelrar...you know exactly where on the planet he is, right?"

"Right," Lenara agreed. "Do not panic. I am just coming into his country's airspace now, excuse me."

Voices crackled into life over the comms, asking Lenara questions Mac had no interest in. He waited until she had finished speaking and begun the descent over a vast area of red landscape that appeared largely uninhabited before he spoke. "Is he nearby or do we have to do more travelling?"

"He is underground."

The *Veena* landed with a gentle *whoosh* noise, and the humming—which Mac barely noticed when it was happening—fell silent. Lenara flicked a few more switches before she left her seat and headed out the cockpit, leaving Mac to follow. They met up with Teevar and Ral and left the ship together. Nerves fluttered in Mac's stomach, though he wasn't really sure why unless it wasn't nerves but excitement.

Lenara seemed to know where she was going, so they followed her towards a large, metal warehouse-like structure, which, when they entered, Mac saw was full of other aircraft and vehicles, some of which had aliens in grey jumpsuits tinkering with them. The aliens themselves appeared almost human, except their skin was orange and hairless, and their eyes were large black orbs. They were obviously used to the comings and goings of off-worlders, because not one of them paid them a blind bit of attention. The acrid smell of engine oil and fuel made Mac cough, and he was pleased when Lenara stopped walking.

A large box with two doors on one side appeared randomly positioned in the warehouse. Lenara tapped something into a console just in front of it, and the doors slid open.

"It's a lift," Mac said, though judging by the others' reactions he figured he was pointing out the obvious. He joined them inside, and the doors slid closed once more. "This is kinda like a mining shaft or something, right?"

"There is no mining here," Lenara said. "The population live underground. In this part of the world, there are often solar flares that make life almost impossible topside."

Mac's stomach flipped with the movement of the lift coming to a stop, and as the doors opened, he gawped at what was in front of him. Far from being dark, the cavern was bright and airy and bustling with activity. Music floated over to him, followed by song and laughter. The place was full of people selling things—taking advantage of newcomers arriving—and Lenara waved away anybody who approached their group.

"This place is amazing." Mac turned back to watch as a large holographic screen near the centre of the cavern flicked through images of people—creatures, aliens, he had no idea—with words written in a language he couldn't decipher scrolling across it.

Teevar tugged his arm. "Best not to watch that."

"Why? What is it?" He glanced back again, but the others were going on without him, so he hurried to catch up.

They passed through the cavern and into a quieter, cooler passageway where there were fewer people and less noise. It was a system of tunnels, some leading into caverns again, others crossing their path. Judging by the fact that Lenara knew *exactly* where she was going, Mac guessed she'd visited before.

They trudged onwards, the lighting along the walls of the tunnel becoming less frequent and fewer people passing, until they came to a curtain covering a round door in the wall.

Lenara raised a hand to stop any of them from proceeding. "Kelrar?" she called.

Mac strained his ears, sure he could hear scuffling behind the curtain. For a moment, nobody answered.

"Lenara?" The curtain drew back, and a man—a venek judging by how similar he looked to Lenara, minus the horns—stood before them. He laughed suddenly and pulled Lenara into a hug, slapping her back.

"It's good to see you too," she murmured.

"Lenara, it might not be safe for you here. Have you seen the 'grams?"

"We won't be here long." She turned and waved a hand at the group. "My companions: Teevar Nok Dimar, Mackenzie Jones, and Ral."

Kelrar's gaze flicked over them only briefly before he looked at Lenara again. "Come inside," he said. "It's private, never fear."

Mac was the last person to enter, and something made him check back over his shoulder to make sure they weren't being followed, but nobody seemed to be paying them any attention.

Inside the little cave was cosy and cluttered. A candle flickered on a table, illuminating parchments and star charts. Behind the table, another round door led off to, presumably, the rest of Kelrar's home. Or office. Or whatever it was.

Mac picked up one of the stone-carved ornaments on one of the many shelves and frowned before he put it down and picked up another.

"Please be careful with those," Kelrar said, shuffling behind the table. "They're very old."

Mac put the ornament down and raised his hands. "Have you heard of Earth?"

"Earth?" Kelrar shook his head and looked to Lenara.

"It is Mackenzie's home," she said. "He wishes to take us there; he has offered us sanctuary."

"Not heard of it." Kelrar made a show of searching through the maps on his desk. "Does it go by another name? Hmm. Haasa, perhaps? I have heard there is a colony of kovans settled on Haasa."

"Okay, first, I'm human, not kovan," Mac said. "Second, no it doesn't have another name. It's in the Milky Way, if that helps."

"Mickyway, mickyway," Kelrar repeated, flicking through his papers once more.

Mac sighed. "He hasn't got a bloody clue," he said to nobody in particular.

Somebody touched the small of his back, the gentlest of touches. He looked at Teevar, who gave him a sympathetic smile and removed his hand. "We'll find it," he said.

"I am sorry," Kelrar said. He straightened up from his maps and beckoned Lenara deeper into the cave where they spoke together in hushed tones.

Ral was fiddling with something that looked like a spiky glass paperweight, and Mac watched as she tested it with her teeth.

"Be careful with that!" Kelrar barked, rounding the table to snatch it from her. "Very dangerous." He clicked his teeth at them and shooed them from the room.

They stood outside, waiting for Lenara. "Dangerous my arse," Mac said. "It was a paperweight." He leaned closer to the curtain, listening. "I bet they're lovers. Or ex-lovers. I bet they're in there now, shagging."

Teevar gave him a quizzical look. "Shagging?"

"I'll show you sometime." He winked and then grinned widely as Teevar turned a very pleasant shade of pink—the context, if not the words, understood.

"They're coming." Ral ushered them out of the way, as the curtain pulled back and Lenara and Kelrar exited the cave. Lenara had a rolled-up star chart in her hand.

"Time to go." She exchanged a look with Kelrar, which Mac was certain was full of sexual tension, and then she walked past them and headed back down the tunnel.

"You've got a map?" Mac asked, hurrying to keep up. "Not to Earth, though, right?"

"Not to Earth," Lenara confirmed. "To a largely uncharted territory. We can be safe there for a while."

"Just a while? Bloody marvellous."

They strode along the tunnel until they emerged into the main cavern once again. Lenara led them all back to the lift, but Mac looked back, not able to resist another look at the holographic screen.

The image moved to show the next person, and Mac had to double take when he recognised Lenara. Symbols he couldn't read scrolled across her picture. Then it changed and showed Teevar. More symbols. And then, himself.

"What the hell?"

Teevar grabbed his arm and pulled him onwards as the lift doors opened. "We have to go now," he said. "Right now."

"What? Is that like a giant wanted poster or something? It is, isn't it? It's a bloody wanted poster!" He just caught sight of the picture changing to one of Ral before Teevar dragged him into the lift and the doors slid shut.

Mac clenched his fists by his side. "Somebody would've seen that. How many times has that scrolled around? I haven't actually done anything!"

"Besides fraud." Teevar offered Mac an apologetic smile.

"Quickly," Lenara said, as the lift slowed and then stopped. "Keep your heads down and keep walking. Don't stop."

"Bollocks," Mac muttered as the doors opened. He fixed his gaze firmly on the floor and followed the others. "I'm not made for this sort of thing. I'm an honest, valued, high-class citizen on my planet. I shouldn't have to put up with this sort of thing. I—"

"Shh!" Lenara hissed.

Somebody shouted at them to stop, and for some unfathomable reason, Lenara stopped.

Mac stood next to Teevar, heart pulsing, as two of the orange-skinned aliens approached them—these ones dressed in matching smart uniforms and not the jumpsuits of their fellows. Ral glanced back at him. "Be ready to run," she said.

*What if they've already clamped the ship?* Mac thought.

"We would like you to come with us, please," one of the aliens said.

"What is this about?" Lenara demanded.

The alien smiled and raised his hands. "Nothing to worry you. Please, no fuss. We just wish to talk to you."

A slight movement from the other alien caught Mac's eye, and he noticed the man's hand slip to a weapon holstered at his side. Without thinking, he yelled, "Run!"

Everything happened at once. He shouted. Lenara lashed out and punched the alien talking to her in the face. Ral dived out of the way as the other alien drew his weapon, and Mac shoved Teevar in front of him to force him into a run.

The aliens yelled at them to stop—the ones working on the spacecrafts turned from their labour to watch. Lenara ran one way; Teevar the other. Ral bounded on top of vehicles, leaping from one to the other as weapons fired around them. Mac raced after Teevar, ducking and weaving. He pulled metal barrels into the path of the alien chasing them and laughed in triumph when the man tripped.

"Stop them." The voice blared into life over loudspeakers, echoing in the warehouse.

Mac cursed as the workers stopped what they were doing and some snatched out at them as they ran past. He could no longer see Lenara. Teevar ran just ahead, and as he dived under the undercarriage of a large, sleek aircraft and emerged out the other side, Ral dropped down beside him.

"Keep going," she shouted. "Go!"

She stopped and he ran on. When he looked back, he saw she was taking on three of the workers who'd piled on top of her.

"Bollocks to this." Mac drew his gun and fired, catching one of Ral's assailants in the leg. She burst free and ran after him.

"The ship!" Teevar yelled. The gangway lowered before them, beckoning them on. Lenara, there before them, hurried inside.

In swift bounds, Ral soon overtook Mac and Teevar. Mac turned to fire off a few more shots, warning their pursuers not to come after them, before he raced up the gangway into the ship.

Lenara smacked the door controls, and the gangway pulled up, shots sparking off the metal.

"Can they shoot us down?" Mac asked as the venek ran off to the cockpit. "Can they? Does this thing have any weapons?"

"No weapons," Teevar said grimly, indicating that they should retreat farther into the ship. "And yes, they can shoot us down."

All three of them joined Lenara in the cockpit and watched as she launched the ship in the air. Orange-skinned aliens scattered all around them, mouthing their anger, some shooting, black orbs blinking. *They only have tiny guns*, Mac thought as they fired uselessly. *We're fine!*

"They are launching a ship," Lenara said, as she pulled on the controls. "Hold on to something."

Mac's first instinct was to hold on to Teevar. Instead, he grabbed the back of the passenger seat as Teevar strapped himself in.

Lenara laughed like a lunatic as she jerked the controls and the ship banked sharply. A bolt of light—gunfire—streaked past them.

"Why the hell are they trying to kill us?" Mac yelled.

"Probably just trying to bring us down," Teevar said. "Or kill us," he added, as more gunfire passed close by.

Mac gripped the seat tight as Lenara threw the ship about as if it was a bumper car. She banked again and the enemy ship grew large in the windscreen, heading straight for them. Mac held his breath. Lenara pulled the controls, and the ship rose sharply, up and over the top of the other and then up, up, through the atmosphere and out into space.

"No weapons, but this thing has a warp drive or something, right?" Mac asked. "Some sort of super speed travel?"

"*Veena* is able to travel faster than light," Lenara said, "but she prefers not to." She looked back to give Mac a brief smile. "Relax. We're not being followed. They've lost us. We're not worth that much to them that they pursue."

"Great." Mac released his hold of the chair and straightened his clothes. "I'll be in my room."

He left the cockpit. Teevar's footsteps pattered out of the room after him. "Wait. Mac?"

Mac didn't stop walking, but he didn't tell Teevar to bugger off either. "I think we need to talk," Mac said. "I could've died today. I could've been shot. Again."

He reached his room and pulled open the door, leaving it ajar for Teevar to join him inside. He fiddled with his hair and then sat on the bed, waiting as Teevar hovered by the door before apparently deciding to join him.

"What have you done that warrants wanted posters and bounty hunters?" Mac asked. "You, the priest."

Tentatively, Teevar sat by his side on the bed and gazed at his hands. "I am ashamed."

Mac gazed at Teevar's profile, again struck by how human he looked. The man's nose was ever-so-slightly upturned. *Perfect.* Mac caught himself smiling and stopped.

"What?" Teevar caught his eye. "You're smiling."

"You looked so serious."

"You asked a serious question." Teevar was smiling too now. Carefully, Mac lifted his hand and touched Teevar's face. When the other man didn't move away, Mac kissed him.

Teevar pulled back and blinked in surprise. "What was that?"

"A kiss. Where I'm from it's what we do to people we like." He kept his hand to Teevar's face, stroked his cheek with his thumb, and then kissed him again. Teevar returned his kiss, his lips warm and gentle, and Mac moved his hand down his face to his chest, past the gold chain, and down—

"Stop." Teevar took hold of Mac's hand and pushed it back to him. His face was red. "I don't know what you think is going to happen, but it must stop."

Mac sighed and flopped back on the bed. "On Earth, people pay to have sex with me."

"Because you are so important?"

Mac laughed. "Yeah. Because I'm so important." He rubbed his face and then sat up again. "No. It's not really seen as a good thing. I provide a service, and that's it. Guys use me at night and then throw me away in the daylight—they wouldn't be seen dead with me. I'm like a...well, I can't think of an analogy. Some sort of tea bag sex vampire."

Teevar stood. "I think we should all get some sleep. Tomorrow we will see where Lenara takes us."

Mac watched him leave. He settled back on the bed again and stared at the ceiling for a while before he got up to get undressed for bed. He wondered again what Teevar had done and fell asleep with him in his dreams.

# Chapter Five

MAC HAD NO idea what the time was, or whether morning had arrived—if there was such a thing as morning in space. He still hadn't figured out the change in time—but the lights came on in his room and woke him up. Grumbling, he showered and dressed and then made his way to the kitchen to find himself something to eat. When he got there, Ral was already rooting through the cupboards. She spun around when he entered and flashed him her teeth.

"Only me," he said, taken aback. "Didn't mean to startle you."

"Where is the meat?" she asked.

Mac shrugged. "Don't ask me, not a bloody clue." He frowned and sidled past her to grab a block of brown food that, when he'd tried some yesterday, tasted vaguely of dates. He found a knife and cut a slice. "Want some?"

"I can't digest that." Ral growled and then turned and left the kitchen, pushing past Teevar on his way in.

"Someone's hangry," Mac commented. Then, when Teevar looked puzzled, "You know. Hungry, angry. Hangry. It's a new thing. You've probably not heard of it."

Teevar smiled a little. He joined Mac in cutting some food for himself and took it to the table. "About last night," he started.

"Already forgotten," Mac said. "That's if you wanted to forget it."

Teevar nodded. "I'm sorry."

"Wish you'd stop apologising." Mac took a seat and munched on his date slice. Teevar was subdued, so he changed the subject of conservation, and Teevar, grateful, perked up.

It wasn't long before Lenara joined them. She fetched her breakfast and sat opposite them at the table. "I know what you really did on Earth," she said.

"Fuck's sake." Mac looked at Teevar, who mouthed *I'm sorry* at him. He turned back to Lenara. "Okay yeah, I lied. I'm not super important, but if I go back with you guys, I soon will be! And you guys will be too. Plus, what better hiding place for you lot than a planet nobody can find?"

"I cannot take you somewhere I don't know how to find," Lenara said. "I'm sorry, little human, but Earth is lost to you."

Mac thumped his fist on the table. "Stop calling me 'little human.' You need to take me back to where you first found me. The kovans got me here; they can take me back."

"Too dangerous." Lenara put a slice of date-loaf between her teeth and chewed slowly. She met Mac's gaze and then turned to Teevar. "Today we enter the Nendus system. Kelrar's star chart covers some of the area, enough to get us in. And after that..." She shrugged. "We will lose ourselves."

Mac pushed his chair back from the table and got up. "I hope you have fun running for the rest of your lives. Drop me off at the nearest planet." He glared at them both and then stomped out of the kitchen.

Mac had almost reached his room when somebody bowled into him from behind and he fell forward, crying out as his hands smacked the floor hard. He struggled and turned himself over, Ral on top of him, her eyes wide.

"I'm hungry," she said.

"Not my problem." Mac squirmed beneath her. "I swear to god I'll bloody shoot you if you don't get off me!"

"Your problem if I eat you," she said, her teeth inches from his face.

Mac managed to get a hold of his gun, and he pushed it into Ral's side. "No one is fucking eating me," he growled. "I'm sick of the whole damn lot of you. I've had enough! Get off!"

Ral looked down at the weapon. Then her eyes cleared and she got off him, her hands raised. "Forgive me. Maybe Teevar or Lenara have something for me."

"Yeah, go ask them." Mac kept his gun trained on her until she turned and disappeared back down the corridor. He sighed deeply and entered his room. He had to get off the ship. He'd find someone else to help him and then...

*I'm so screwed.*

TIME PASSED. MAC dozed off. He woke with a start when somebody hammered on his door, and he got up to wrench it open. "What?"

Teevar pushed into the room and closed the door behind him. "Slight change of plan," he said. "We need to stop running for a bit. Ral's...feral. We need to find the nearest inhabited planet and stock up on supplies."

"Great, and you can leave me there."

"What? No!"

"I mean it, Teevar. I'm pissed off with all this. Lenara should've left me where she found me."

"I don't want you to go."

Mac laughed. "And why the hell not?" he asked. "What does it matter to you what I do?"

"I like you."

"Big fucking deal."

"I like you more than I should."

Mac shook his head. He stood inches from Teevar and glared at him, fists clenched at his side. "I don't care. I am *done* with this. I—"

Teevar grabbed his face and kissed him. It was awkward at first, Teevar pressing a little harder than he should, but Mac, angry, kissed him back. They fell against the wall together, Teevar fighting with Mac's clothes now. Mac shrugged his top off and reached his hands inside Teevar's loose-fitting pants, he pulled back and grinned triumphantly when he felt Teevar was already hard.

"You feel human," he said.

Teevar's face was flushed red, though Mac didn't know whether from arousal or embarrassment. Or both. They kissed again, and Teevar pushed Mac down onto the bed before climbing on top of him. "I shouldn't do this," he breathed.

"But you want to." Mac reached for Teevar's dick again and stroked it, causing the other man to groan.

His mind made up, Teevar pulled back long enough to yank Mac's trousers down, take hold of his legs, and flip him over. Mac felt Teevar's weight press down on him. *I'm about to be fucked by an alien.* The thought turned him on, and he arched his back as Teevar's cock pushed inside him.

"Yes," he muttered, reaching back to pull Teevar closer. It hurt at first without preparation, and Teevar was rough, but Mac's mouth ran dry, and he planted his face in the pillow to stifle his moans.

When they finished, Teevar stayed over him for a moment or two, his breathing heavy before rolling off and lay by his side.

"I'm sorry," he said, as Mac turned over. "Did I hurt you?"

"Nah. You made me come all over my bed though. You're going to have to show me where the laundry room is."

Teevar laughed. "By the Gods, I'm so sorry," he said again.

"Stop apologising." Mac propped himself up on an elbow and gazed at Teevar. "Tell me what you did?"

"It will make you hate me," Teevar said, his voice soft as he looked away.

Mac said nothing. He waited for Teevar to speak, and a long enough time passed that he thought that was the end of the conversation. The hum of the engines changed enough for Mac to recognise they were nearing a planet.

"I killed someone."

Mac raised his eyebrows. "*You* killed someone?"

"In my country, for two males to do what we just did, it is illegal. I...had a relationship with a young man who delivered food to our temple." He swallowed hard. "We were seen. And I had to protect us. I had to stop word getting out."

"You killed the person who caught you."

"Yes." Teevar met his gaze briefly, his eyes full of shame. He quickly looked away and got out of bed to grab his clothes. "I have to go. I need to see where Lenara's taking us."

"Teevar, wait. It's okay, you know. I don't hate you."

Teevar gripped the gold pendant around his neck. "You should." He hesitated, and then turned and left the room.

Mac sighed. He got up to have a quick shower before they landed.

FOR A MOMENT, Mac had to shield his eyes against the sun as he exited *Veena* with the others. The area they'd landed in looked surprisingly like the English countryside. He laughed to himself, and had he not seen the planet before they'd entered the atmosphere, he would've easily believed he was back on Earth.

By his side, Ral was spun out and twitchy, her ears twisting and turning in all directions. "Where is civilisation?" she asked. "Where do we get supplies?"

"There is a lake," Lenara said. "We fish."

"Great. Bloody hate fishing." Mac broke free from the group and wandered down to the lake on his own. He removed his shoes and smiled at the soft grass under his feet. *Feels like Earth.* Maybe it wouldn't be so bad if he stayed there. He could build some sort of hut, hunt and fish, live like a caveman.

He groaned. No electricity? No running hot water? No men. No women! He walked along the lake, glancing back to see the others looking like they were having an argument about how to fish before Ral jumped into the lake and dived under.

"Bloody aliens," he muttered. He stopped to pick up a flat stone and skimmed it across the lake's surface. The activity enveloped him for a while, so much that he jumped in surprise when Teevar joined him.

"Is it a game?" Teevar asked.

Mac smiled. "Yeah," he said. "I guess so. You have to throw the stone and see how many times you can get it to skip across the water."

"Show me?"

"First you need to find a good flat stone." Mac picked one up and showed Teevar. "Then you face the water, work out your angle, and..." He threw the stone and it bounced three times across the lake's surface before it sank.

Teevar smiled. "Let me try." He looked around and chose a large flat stone by his foot, then after giving Mac a nervous grin, he threw it into the water.

Mac laughed. "That was rubbish! Look." He picked up another stone, gave it to Teevar, and then wrapped his hand around the kovan's closed fist. "Like this," he murmured. "Drop your shoulder. That's it. Then flick your wrist—aim across the surface of the water."

He stepped back and Teevar threw the stone, sending it skipping three times across the lake. "Yes!"

"You're a natural." He and Teevar gazed at one another, until Teevar looked away. Sensing the other man was too embarrassed for public shows of affection, Mac nodded back to the girls instead. "They'll never catch anything like that."

Ral burst from the lake, puffing and blowing. She shook before diving under again. Lenara stood in the shallows, her hands in the water.

"You could help," Lenara called.

Just as Mac opened his mouth to protest, Ral surfaced again, a fish in her hands. She rose up and waded back to the shore. The fish was black and had odd long fins and a flat, dolphin-like tail. It looked more like a bird than a fish, and as Mac and Teevar wandered back to the girls, Mac decided he didn't want to try it.

"Make fire," Ral told Teevar, before smacking the fish against a rock. "That one's mine; nobody touch it." She eyed them both suspiciously and then returned to the lake.

Mac helped Teevar gather sticks and kindling for the fire and then sat back on the ground to watch him light it.

"This place," he said, "it reminds me of Earth."

Teevar looked up from striking two stones together. "It does? Earth must be very beautiful."

"Parts of it. I could probably live here, you know. If we could just find some civilisation."

"I don't think you should leave us," Teevar said. A spark flew from the stones and landed amongst the kindling, and he crouched down to breathe it into life.

Mac folded his arms. He didn't really want to stay there with no people around. He wasn't cut out for a hermit lifestyle. He jumped when Lenara threw a fish in front of him.

"Can you gut fish?" she asked.

"No," Mac said, frowning.

"Then you can learn." She sat by his side and handed him a knife.

Sighing deeply and screwing up his nose at the idea of fish guts on his hands, Mac took the knife. He caught the look Teevar gave him, and not wanting to look too much like an ineffectual idiot in front of him, he reached for the fish.

It flapped and flopped about when he touched it, and he cried out and jumped up. "I thought you'd killed it!"

Lenara laughed, and Teevar grinned at him.

"Yeah, very funny." Mac took his seat again as Lenara took the knife from him and quickly decapitated the fish. She set about gutting it as Ral, dripping wet, flopped down beside the fire with another fish.

"Teevar, do you remember our first meal together?" Lenara asked.

"Yes. We were orbiting my planet. I was...frightened, and tense. I didn't want to eat."

"I made us sweet gorshac. My speciality."

Teevar chuckled. "You burnt it. I thought the whole ship would go up in flames." He looked at Mac and smiled. "Lenara had made such an effort that I ate it anyway. It was horrible."

Lenara nodded. Mac imagined the fish would be pretty damn horrible too, but Teevar began cooking, and despite how foul the creatures looked, the smell soon made his stomach rumble. He didn't refuse a portion when it was passed around.

Once everybody had finished eating, they lounged by the lake content to do nothing but relax and take in the scenery. Ral stretched out by the fire and slept, and Lenara went to fetch her star charts to pore over.

Teevar got up and sat very close to Mac. "Still want to stay?" he asked quietly.

Mac shrugged. "No point. I'd get bored very quickly."

They fell silent, and Mac stared into the flames, listening to the fire crackle and pop. After a while, he realised that was the *only* sound he could hear, and he nudged Teevar.

"It's quiet," he whispered.

"Hmm?" Teevar had been dozing. He yawned and sat up a little straighter. "Did you want to sneak off?"

Mac was tempted for a moment until a *plop* from the lake made him take notice. "Something's weird," he said. "Can't you feel it? My spider sense is tingling."

"Spider...?"

Mac waved a hand and got to his feet, staring at the water. "Never mind. Lenara, you hear that?"

"Hear what?"

"Exactly."

Something about Mac's tone must've told Lenara to take him seriously, because she drew her weapon and held it low. The three of them stared at the lake.

"We should wake Ral," Teevar whispered, edging forwards to kneel beside the lupa.

Suddenly, the lake's surface erupted and a scaled *creature* burst forth. It was human in shape, but had frilled gills at the side of its head and large fish-like eyes, no nose, and no lips. It opened its mouth to reveal needle teeth, and it hissed at them.

Ral woke with a start, turned to spot the creature, and scrabbled away. "What is that?"

"It doesn't look friendly," Mac commented, pulling Teevar back to him and pointing his gun at the creature. "I mean, should we shoot it or...?"

For a reply, Lenara fired her weapon, but the creature dived back into the lake. They didn't even have time to hope it'd been frightened away before it emerged again, closer still and angrier looking. It came at them, fast, and Mac turned to race back to the ship only to find there were more of them, appearing as if from nowhere and stopping their retreat.

"This way," Teevar gasped, and he ran alongside the lake, looking back to make sure the others were with him.

Mac ran, and Ral too. Lenara fired another shot before racing after them. The ground was soft beneath Mac's bare feet, luckily, and he soon caught up with Teevar. He needed his breath for running so, he didn't speak. The creatures swarmed and came after them—five, no, he looked again and saw six—six of them, awkward on the land but no slower for it. They ran alongside the lake and then Ral, in the lead, peeled off and headed towards a dense swath of trees.

"We won't make it!" Teevar called. "We—" He tripped and cried out, and it took only a moment before the first creature was on him. "Mac!"

Mac half-turned and then came to an abrupt halt. He watched in horror as Teevar raised a hand to fend off the creature, only for it to sink its teeth into his arm.

Without thinking, he aimed his gun and fired. Black blood and gore exploded from the creature's head as his bolt hit. Teevar struggled free, but Mac barely noticed. His vision narrowed and his focus sharpened. He aimed at the next creature and squeezed the trigger again.

Lenara joined him now and took aim, hitting another in the chest.

*Thump, thump, thump.* Mac's heart sounded loud in his ears. He couldn't hear anything else. He fired again and again, and it was only when all the creatures were down that he could hear himself screaming.

He dropped his weapon and fell to his knees. "Teevar," he muttered.

"I'm here, I'm here." Teevar came to him and wrapped his arms around him. "They're dead. They're all dead."

Mac stared at the corpses and nodded dumbly.

"You did well." Lenara patted his shoulder. She holstered her gun and went to nudge one of the bodies with her boot. She returned to them shortly after and nodded at Teevar's arm. "Are you hurt badly?"

Teevar pulled back and Mac stared at the blood on his arm. "Not...too badly." He touched Mac's face and stood up. "We should head back. We don't know how many more of those things there are. Where's Ral?"

Mac blinked. He gazed at his fallen weapon before reaching for it and tucking it back where it belonged. He tried to ignore the corpses as he got to his feet. "She ran," he said. "She's gone."

# Chapter Six

THE FOREST WAS dark and the ground thick with fallen leaves. Mac shivered and his mind wandered to images of other creatures hiding behind trees or in the bushes. At that point, he didn't really care where Ral was.

"Ral?" Teevar called. He had a hand pressed around the wound to his arm as if it hurt more than he was letting on. "It's safe. You can come out!"

"We're heading back to the *Veena*," Lenara added. "We will leave without you."

"Don't say that," Teevar said. "Ral? Where are you?"

Mac looked dazedly back over his shoulder, back to the open where the bodies lay in the sun.

"Are you okay?" Teevar asked, and he nodded vaguely.

They ventured a little deeper into the forest. Somewhere, an animal called a strange chattering chirp before another answered it. Wind stirred the leaves and sent more of them spinning to the ground.

"Are your spider senses um...doing anything?" Teevar asked.

Mac laughed a little. "No." He reached for Teevar's hand and gave it a squeeze. "No, it's fine." He tapped his cheeks to wake himself up and to shift some of the tingling in his skin. Then he cleared his throat and called out, "Ral? Come out, you coward!"

Lenara raised an eyebrow at him. "Is that wise? One does not usually refer to a lupa as a coward."

"I don't give a tiny rat's arse." Mac stomped ahead and looked all around. "Ral? Get your arse out here or we'll damn well leave you to the bloody fish people! Come out, you bloody *coward*!"

There was a snarl, and then something heavy hit Mac from above and knocked him to the ground. He lashed out and shoved Ral away, even though she bared her teeth at him.

"I am no coward," she said.

"You ran," Mac snapped. "What else would you call it?" He got up and brushed leaf litter and dirt from his clothes.

Ral's ears lay flat on her head. She glared at Mac a moment longer, glanced at Lenara and Teevar, and then lowered her gaze. "You're right. I'm sorry. I...those things..."

"Let's just get back to the ship, eh?" Mac turned away. "I don't fancy hanging around here much longer."

They made their way back to the *Veena* as quickly as possible and boarded the ship with a quick look back to make sure no more lake creatures were after them. Once inside, Lenara headed off to the cockpit and Mac took Teevar to the medical room.

"I can see to this," Teevar said, and Mac wondered if he wasn't trusted with any of the equipment. Which, given he didn't know how to use any of it, was fair enough.

He leaned against the wall and watched as Teevar rolled back his sleeve with a wince. "What were those things? They don't have venomous bites or anything, right?"

"No idea. And I hope not." Teevar gave him a brief smile. He cleaned his wound and then used the same implement he used on Mac to seal it.

"I thought they had you," Mac said.

"I thought so too. Thank you for saving me."

Mac scratched the back of his head. "S'all right. Don't make a habit of getting in trouble though, eh? I'm not cut out for heroics."

Teevar approached Mac and took hold of his hands. "I think you're more capable than you know."

"Better shot than I thought anyway." He squeezed Teevar's hands and then let him go.


THEY DRIFTED IN space for a few days until Lenara made a stop at a commerce outpost to collect supplies. She noted that the extra money they had was running low and if they didn't want to dig into what they had for the bounty hunters, they needed currency from somewhere. Which meant they had to find work.

Mac asked why they couldn't spend the money they had and screw the bloody bounty hunters. As far as he was concerned, running seemed to be going quite well. They took a vote, two—Lenara and Teevar—for saving the money and two against.

They sat together at the table in the kitchen with Lenara's star charts spread before them. Mac was bored and didn't understand what he was looking at, and he drummed his fingers distractedly.

"Why is it uncharted territory when we have charts?" he asked. "Place looks bloody full of planets."

Lenara gave him a dark look. "Most of these are not planets. There is only a very small area covered with these maps and we only have them because of Kelrar's expertise."

"Did you and he have a thing?"

"A thing?"

Mac grinned. "Yeah. You know. A sex thing."

"Sex thing?"

Mac rolled his eyes. "Do I have to spell it out?" He made an 'O' with his thumb and forefinger, and pushed his index finger through the hole. "You've fucked him?"

"You mean like you and Teevar."

"Well, not *quite* like that..."

"How do you know about that?" Teevar demanded, his face red. "I mean...we haven't. I'm not..."

"You think I don't know what goes on in my ship?" Lenara asked. She waved a hand. "I know. Besides, you two are always touching each other nowadays. It is plain to see."

Ral looked from Lenara, to Mac and Teevar. "I hadn't noticed if that makes you feel better."

Mac shrugged. Teevar got to his feet abruptly and left the table, causing Mac to sigh and follow after him. He caught up with the kovan in the corridor, and reached for his hand. "You don't need to hide it here," he said. "Nobody cares."

"*I* care."

"Are you ashamed of me?"

"I am only ashamed of myself." Teevar pulled his hand free and turned his back to Mac. He walked down the corridor and disappeared into his room to hide away.

Mac didn't care for chasing after him. He turned to head back to the girls when he heard coughing coming from Teevar's room. He hesitated and was about to go back to knock on the door when the coughing stopped. Frowning, he turned away.

"Right," he said, rejoining Lenara and Ral. "Where are we going?"

Ral grinned her pointed teeth at him and touched a dot on the map. "Iskaba," she said. "The party planet."

# Chapter Seven

IT WAS DARK on Iskaba, and buildings lit by artificial lights towered over them. The place bustled with life—all sorts of life—and the group had to keep close to each other and squeeze through the crowds to get anywhere. Smoke from street sellers' cook pots stung Mac's eyes, and behind him, Teevar coughed and spluttered.

"What sort of work are we going to be doing, exactly?" Mac asked.

"Whatever you can get," Lenara replied. "Steal if you're good enough to get away with it." She stopped walking and stepped off the main street into a side alley, where she then handed each of them a small metal device. "To contact each other," she explained. "Just touch it and talk and we will hear you. Good luck."

Ral was the first to head away, keen to explore, and Lenara soon left them also. Mac slipped his communications device into his pocket and looked at Teevar. "Do you want to split up, or...?"

"I think we should stay together." Teevar's brows knit together in a serious frown. "We can find work serving, or I can give sermons. I don't think you should...uh...I don't think you should do the work you did on Earth."

"Jealous? Don't worry, I don't really fancy it here. I mean, I saw a guy with tentacles back there, and you just don't know what he'd be doing with those things."

Teevar laughed. He glanced over his shoulder to make sure nobody was watching and then kissed Mac on the lips. "We'll do fine," he said. "Come on."

They walked back to the main street again, content in each other's company for the moment and to do nothing but take in the sights. Eventually Mac, following the sound of music, led them to a bar.

Inside, were it not for the odd-looking people mingling on the dance floor, or the strange otherworldly music, it could've been a bar lifted straight out of London. Mac pulled Teevar with him across the room to the bar at the back, where a very round woman with six arms was serving several people at once.

"I'm not sure they need anybody else working here," Teevar said.

"Who said anything about work? I'm getting us some drinks." He raised his hand to get the server's attention, and she turned two sets of her eyes—she had six of those as well—towards him.

"Yes?"

"Okay, I'll have..." Mac looked around and pointed at the guy standing at the other end of the bar. "...two of those orange things, please."

The woman reached behind her into a cabinet, barely moving her body, and took out two bottles which she slid across the bar to Mac. "Six boule."

"Six? Is that to match your pretty eyes? How about you knock off a couple for a pair of handsome young kovans, eh?" Mac winked at her and she blinked each eye independently in return.

"Six boule," she said again, though she turned her body towards him now, giving him her full attention. "You think my eyes are pretty?"

"Uh huh." Mac fished about in his pocket for the coins and placed them on the bar. "Very pretty. Like jewels. You're a very attractive woman in general. Why, if I wasn't married I'd be tempted to ask for your hand."

"My hand?"

"In marriage."

The woman chuckled, a sound which bubbled in her throat and spilled out between her lips. Mac smiled as she tapped his cheek. "You are lying," she said. "But I like it. You come back for your next drink free."

"I most definitely will." Mac flashed her a wide grin and then clinked his bottle against Teevar's before turning away with him to dance.

"You are terrible," Teevar said, though he was smiling.

"It worked, didn't it?" Mac slugged back a mouthful of his drink and pulled a face. The liquid tasted like the smell of gasoline and burned his throat when he swallowed. "This is awful!"

"I don't really drink this sort of thing," Teevar admitted, clutching the bottle awkwardly in his hands.

"I'll drink it," Mac said, taking the bottle from him. "Go and order something you like."

He kissed Teevar and watched as he headed back to the bar. When he turned around, a young woman stood before him. She looked human, and so he presumed her to be kovan. She had blonde hair and striking green eyes and wore a *very* low-cut top which Mac just couldn't help looking down.

"Hi," he said. He drank another mouthful and pulled his gaze up from her cleavage. "Ethan Smith. Nice to meet you."

"Eesha Dak Lomar," she replied. "Don't I know you?"

"Highly unlikely," Mac said. He handed her Teevar's bottle, and she took it with a smile.

"Dance with me?" she asked, and before he could protest—not that he wanted to—she pulled him deeper into the crowd.

Mac danced and drank the orange liquid until his head spun. Music pulsed and throbbed in his veins, the beat eventually matching his heart. Eesha was very close to him, and she smelled of cinnamon and sex.

"Ethan Smith is a strange name," she said, leaning close to his ear. "You must be from Portensia."

"That's right."

Eesha pulled back and smiled, her lips red and swollen. "Very strange." She laughed, tilting her chin back so that Mac's gaze drew once more to her bosom. "I like it."

"Yeah? E*esha*, E*than* sounds good together, right?" He hooked an arm around her waist and drew her closer still. She touched her collar bone, drawing his eye down.

Mac blinked dazedly and wondered what it would be like to kiss her. *Don't do it, Mac.* His skin tingled.

"Sounds very good," Eesha commented, leaning close. "Come with me." She smiled again, took his hand and led him from the room.

Mac had to screw his eyes shut as Eesha took him into a room that was too bright at first. She threw him down on to a pile of cushions and he laughed as his drink slopped over his hand.

"Careful!" He put the bottle down and sat up as Eesha straddled him. "Are you trying to take advantage of me?" A tiny voice at the back of his mind told him he needed to stop, but a louder, drunker voice told him to shut the hell up; Eesha was hot. He moaned when she slipped her cool hand inside his pants. "I'm a bit drunk," he whispered.

"I know," Eesha replied. She pushed him back again and ripped his shirt open, tracing her hands over his chest. Mac squinted up at her, the light—or maybe his drink—making his head pound.

"I've seen your picture," Eesha said, her mouth close to his ear, her breath hot on his skin. "You robbed the skreens." She pushed him back roughly as he tried to get up, and sucked his nipple.

"They gave me their money," Mac said, gasping when he felt her teeth. "I didn't rob them, exactly."

He closed his eyes as Eesha worked on his other nipple and tried to ignore the room spinning around him. He opened his mouth as she grabbed his cock again.

"What have you done with the money?" she asked.

"What?"

"Where is the money?"

"Oh. It's, uh..." He swallowed hard and opened his eyes, as she pumped him with her fist.

"Don't you want me?"

"Yes. I mean no. No. Well, yes, I do, but I shouldn't."

"Tell me where the money is. You must be clever to have hidden it from the skreens."

She'd stopped touching him. "It's not really hidden," Mac said, sitting up on his elbows, his throat dry. "It's just in our ship."

"What's your ship's name?"

Mac opened his mouth to answer, when the door to the room burst open and music flooded in before it was quickly closed out again. Teevar gaped at him. "Somebody told me you'd come in here," he said. "Enjoying yourself?"

Mac cursed and shoved Eesha off. "Teevar! I was just...I was...We were..."

"Can't think of a lie, Mac?" Teevar asked.

"Hey, I wasn't going to lie! You've got the complete wrong end of the stick here. You've put two and two together and come up with five. We were just—"

"My religion doesn't make me naïve," Teevar hissed. He clutched his gold pendant in his fist and then he shook his head and turned and left the room.

Mac hurried to his feet, arranged his clothes back in place, and ignoring Eesha, dashed out after Teevar. He couldn't see him through the crowd and he cursed again. He pushed his way through to the bar and tapped the bar surface urgently until the server turned to him.

"Have you seen my friend?" he asked. "The guy I came in with? Which way did he go?"

"Out," the woman said, pointing towards the door. "He's gone out."

He nodded his thanks and ran outside, the cool air hitting him and making him sober up pretty quickly. *Idiot*, he told himself. *Stupid, bloody idiot.*

"Teevar?" he called.

He chose a direction and set off, scanning faces and peering over heads. It wasn't until he'd almost reached the *Veena* again that he remembered the device Lenara had given him. He stopped and sat on a low wall, pulling the device from his pocket. He pressed the button and wondered if everybody would hear him, or just the person he wished to speak to.

"Teevar?" he tried.

People walked past him, ignoring him, and a cool breeze made him shiver. He looked over his shoulder when he had a feeling of someone watching him, but nobody lurked in the shadows.

"Teevar? I'm sorry, okay. I was drunk. That orange stuff is obviously not safe for human consumption."

He waited but nobody replied. He rubbed his face, inspected the little metal device and, realising it had a pin on it, he attached it to his shirt. "Teevar, can you meet me back at the *Veena*, and we'll talk about this? I'm going there now, okay? I'll see you there."

He walked back to the ship and tapped in the code Lenara had told him to open the door, vaguely surprised it worked and she hadn't given him a false number. He clambered up the gangway and sat at the top to wait, wondering if Teevar would make him wait all night.

It wasn't long before Eesha appeared. She stood at the bottom of the gangway, her hands on her hips, looking so like one of his ex-girlfriends that his heart skipped. He got to his feet and jabbed a finger at her.

"You can bugger off right now!"

"I can't do that, *Mac*." She walked up the gangway, hips sashaying as if she were a femme fatale straight out of a movie.

Mac reached for his gun, cursing when he realised it was gone.

"Looking for this?" Eesha asked, drawing the weapon and pointing it at him. "Take me to the money now, and I won't turn you in."

"Hey, I earned that money fair and square. Go and pull your own scam."

"I did. You." She pressed the gun into his stomach when she reached him. "Take me to the money."

Mac had his hands in the air. He wondered if he'd be quick enough to disarm her before she pulled the trigger and decided not to risk it. Instead, he ran through excuses in his head: *we lost the money; we spent the money; I don't know where it is.*

Feet scuffed behind Eesha and she spun around. Lenara stood at the bottom of the gangway, a gun pointed at the kovan. "You left your comms on, Mac," she said.

"Alien technology," Mac said, shrugging.

Eesha moved quickly, grabbing Mac and pulling him close to her. She pushed the gun against his neck. "Come any closer and I shoot him," she warned.

"Go ahead," Lenara said. "Once he is dead, I shoot you."

"Hey!" Mac tried to pull away from Eesha, but she held him tight. "Don't anybody shoot me!"

"Just give me the money and I walk away. I won't let anybody know you're here."

Lenara clicked her teeth. "I do not trust you," she said. "If we give you the money, you will take it *and* the reward when you turn us in."

"How does she even know who we are?" Mac asked. "What's the bloody point in running to supposedly uncharted planets, when people still find us! I can't beli—"

Eesha grabbed him and threw him down the gangway where he fell into Lenara—she pushed him aside, and he had just enough time to register nothing was broken as Eesha sprinted into the ship with Lenara hot on her heels.

Cursing, Mac pulled himself up and dashed after them both. Inside, the ship was quiet. He strained to listen, half-expecting Eesha to jump out from somewhere and shoot him dead. Then he heard a shout, and he ran up the stairs after it.

"Lenara?" he called. He pulled open the door and stopped in the corridor to see the venek standing over Eesha—blood pumped from a wound in the kovan's thigh. "You shot her?"

"I meant to kill her," Lenara replied. "I will rectify that."

"Wait!" Mac placed himself firmly between Eesha and Lenara and raised his hands. "Don't kill her."

"She will betray us," Lenara said. "She cannot live."

"If you kill her, we're going to have a corpse to deal with. We'll probably be found out, and knowing our luck, we'll all be done for murder. Now just help me tie her up or something." He snatched up his gun from where Eesha had dropped it and then gave Lenara a pointed look when she was slow to move.

Lenara rolled her eyes. "Take her to the medical bay and fix her up. I will fetch some rope."

"Right." Mac hooked Eesha's arm around his shoulders and hauled her to her feet, ignoring her pained cry. "You are a pain in the arse," he told her. "You should've stayed out of this."

"I saw an opportunity, and I took it," Eesha replied. "It's not my fault if you are stupid. Ow!"

Mac practically dumped her on the bed in the medical bay before searching around for the implements he'd seen Teevar use to heal his wounds. "I'm going to need you to keep *very* still." He tore the material away from Eesha's wound, frowned over the laser device for a moment, and then held it as if it were a pen and pointed it at the wound. A red beam worked to knit the skin together, and Eesha grit her teeth against the pain.

Once it was done, Lenara joined them, thrusting rope at Mac and instructing him to tie Eesha up. She touched her comms device. "Ral, Teevar. Come back to the *Veena* as soon as you can. We need to leave."

"What are you going to do with me?" Eesha asked. "You can't keep me prisoner."

"We'll just dump you off at the next planet," Mac said, looking back at Lenara. "Right?"

Lenara nodded. "Or flush you into space."

Mac tightened the ropes around Eesha's wrists and tied her ankles too so that she couldn't walk. He straightened up. "Sorted. Let's go."

He went to stand by the open door, waiting for the others. Ral arrived first and she gave him a quizzical look before he sent her to Lenara for an explanation. He stared out towards the city, willing Teevar to appear.

*What if he doesn't come back? What if something's happened to him?* His chest tightened at the thought, and he scratched the back of his head as if he could claw away the worry.

The night drew in and grew ever colder. He felt like he'd waited an age before he spotted Teevar walking towards him.

"Hey!" He ran down the gangway to greet him. "I was getting concerned. We've got to scarper—people here know who we are."

Teevar nodded. "I've seen the 'grams." He stalked past Mac and up into the ship. "Don't speak to me again, Mackenzie. Not for a while."

Mac opened his mouth to protest, to beg forgiveness, or say it wasn't his fault. Instead he sighed, followed Teevar inside, and closed up the door. He touched his comms device. "All aboard, Lenara. We can go now."

# Chapter Eight

MAC LAY IN his room and tried not to think about Eesha, although the more he tried not to, the more he did. He didn't know how long it'd take them to reach the next planet, but he wanted Eesha gone. With her there, it was a constant reminder of what he'd done, and he didn't know how much of Teevar's silent treatment he could take.

The only positive that came out of the whole trip was that Ral had managed to steal about a hundred boule in a grab-and-run from one of the street vendors. Not much, but it'd do for the moment.

Mac sighed. Why did it matter if he'd almost slept with Eesha? As far as he was aware, he and Teevar weren't exclusive. They weren't even a couple, were they? It shouldn't *matter*. But the look on Teevar's face when he'd caught them haunted him, and he realised that it *did* matter, and that thought unsettled him.

Determined, he got up and left his room, deciding he'd talk to Teevar and clear the air between them. He paused outside the kovan's room, frowning at the coughing coming from inside.

"Teevar?"

"Go away."

More coughing. Mac reached for the handle and, finding the door unlocked, let himself into the room. Teevar turned away quickly, but not before Mac had spotted the blood on the handkerchief he coughed into.

"Are you okay?"

"I am *fine*."

"You don't look fine." He touched Teevar's shoulder, but the kovan shrugged him off. "Teevar, that's blood."

"I...it's nothing. Go and worry over Eesha." Teevar sat on his bed, held a hand to his chest, and took some deep breaths. He glared at Mac. "You shouldn't be in here."

"Please, it's not as if I've never been in here before. Probably the first time I've been in here and seen you in so many clothes, though."

Teevar dabbed his lips with the handkerchief. "Are all members of your species like you? You mate with males and females."

"No. Where I'm from, it's called being bisexual. You don't have bisexual people on your planet?" Tentatively, he sat himself beside Teevar on the bed and once more frowned at the handkerchief.

"On my planet, males and females only mate with each other."

Mac smiled a little. "Clearly not true."

Teevar shook his head. "Then I don't know. In other countries, I have heard that two males and two females can become lovers. Anything else, I don't know."

"I am sorry, you know," Mac said. "I didn't think. Somebody once told me I'm ruled by my dick. It's true, I guess. I should, uh…I should engage my brain more often."

Teevar coughed again, doubling over and hacking violently into the handkerchief. Mac rubbed his back, and then poured Teevar a drink.

"You're not okay," he said. "You're coughing up blood."

"I just need rest." Teevar's voice came out hoarse. "Please, Mac. I need to sleep now."

Reluctantly, Mac left the room. He waited outside a moment, but Teevar's coughing fit had passed and all was quiet.

THE NEXT DAY, the four of them sat together for breakfast and Mac was pleased to note Teevar looked a little brighter. He wanted to ask how he was feeling, but didn't in case it embarrassed him in front of the girls. Teevar didn't stay with them for long, soon excusing himself to take food to Eesha.

*Eesha.* Mac had almost forgotten she was still there. He pushed his food around his plate and then passed it over to Ral when she asked if he was going to eat it. He got up and left without a word, making his way to the star room where he gazed out into the black.

Maybe Lenara would know what was up with Teevar—the two had known each other the longest, maybe she knew if he had allergies, or….

Mac rubbed his face. What was the disease on Earth where people coughed up blood? It was something people used to die off in the olden days, he was sure of that. He wished he'd paid more attention in history class. He searched his brain, but it was beyond him.

A thought struck him, and he made his way to where Eesha was being held in the medical bay. *She* would know—she and Teevar were the same species. He waited outside the room for a moment and listened in case Teevar was still in with her. Everything was quiet, so he stepped inside.

Eesha sat up and glared at him. "What do you want?"

"Do you know anything about kovan illnesses?"

"Do I look like a doctor?"

Mac folded his arms. "Teevar's coughing up blood. Do you know anything about that or not? I'm worried about him."

Eesha muttered a curse that didn't quite translate. "He's as good as dead," she said. "I am too now that I've been exposed!" She cursed again.

Unsettled, Mac uncrossed his arms and approached Eesha. "What do you mean? What's wrong with him?"

"Sounds like he has the rotten blood. He will keep coughing blood—vomiting blood, shitting blood—until he's dried up." She struggled violently against the ropes and then screamed in annoyance. "Let me out of here!"

Mac backed up, turned, and ran from the medical bay. He hammered on Teevar's door and opened it when he received no answer, but the room was empty. He dashed down the corridor and bumped into Ral.

"Have you seen Teevar?"

"Praying," she said. "Why—"

Mac raced to the star room and burst inside, not caring if he interrupted Teevar's prayers. Teevar, surrounded by his incense, opened his eyes and frowned at Mac. "I usually like to conduct my prayers in private," he said.

"Are you dying?" Mac demanded.

Teevar laughed a little. "Excuse me?"

"The blood. You're coughing up blood. I spoke to Eesha—she mentioned rotten blood."

"I have never heard of that." Teevar blew out his candles and got to his feet. "She's trying to scare you, Mac. Have you not learnt to keep away from her yet?"

Mac took hold of Teevar's arm to stop him passing by. "No," he said. "She was *scared*. She was telling the truth! She said you have the rotten blood, and she said she can get it too. How do we fix this?"

Teevar took Mac's hand gently and freed his arm. "I am not going to die," he said. "And I am praying for better health."

Mac almost laughed. Why wasn't Teevar worried? God knows, he was. So worried that he felt sick to his stomach. He shook his head. "You need medical help. I'll speak to Lenara and see if we can find an inhabited planet. There's bound to be a doctor somewhere."

Teevar sighed. "If it makes you feel better." He inclined his head and left the room.

"It'll make you feel better!" Mac called after him. *Praying*, he thought. *Fat lot of good that'll do.*

MAC JOINED LENARA in the cockpit and sat by her side. Eventually he said, "Teevar's sick."

"I know."

"We need to find a planet with people."

"I know that, too."

Mac looked over at the venek. Her brow had furrowed into a frown. "Are we anywhere near a planet?" he asked.

Lenara gave an almost imperceptible shake of her head. "According to Kelrar's charts, we should've passed a dead star, but I have not seen it."

"And what does that mean?"

"Either the maps are wrong, or we are lost."

"We're lost?" Mac laughed. "Well, isn't that bloody fantastic! We're lost in space. Jesus bloody Christ."

Lenara glanced at him. "I do not know this Jesus Bloody Christ."

"No," Mac agreed. He sighed and then got to his feet, laying a hand on Lenara's shoulder. "Find somewhere. Please."

She nodded, and he left the cockpit. He wandered back to his room and grabbed the electronic notepad he'd bought himself on the commerce moon. He'd intended to keep a diary of all the extraordinary things he'd seen and then sell his story back on Earth, but so far all he'd done was doodle a dick pic and written the words *The Amazing Adventures of Mackenzie Jones: Space Mac.*

He made his way to Teevar's room and knocked on the door.

"Who is it?"

"Mac."

He waited. The door clicked unlocked, and he took that as permission to enter. "Hey," he said, looking at Teevar sitting on the bed. "How are you feeling?"

"Fine. Thank you."

Mac, not about to let Teevar's coolness deter him, joined him on the bed and made himself comfy. "Right." Mac turned on the notepad. "I thought I'd show you Earth."

Teevar raised his eyebrows. "I know you're not great with alien technology, but you do know what that thing does, don't you?"

"'Course." Mac grinned. He gave Teevar's shoulder a playful nudge and turned his attention back to the pad. "Just pay attention."

Carefully, he ran his index finger over the pad, tracing the shape of Earth and the rough, probably terribly inaccurate, outlines of the countries. The pad brought up colours to his fingertips and he tapped them into the shapes, blue and green. He drew the yellow sun and Earth's moon. Teevar was quiet, watching him. Mac swiped the page and started on the next.

"This is my car," he said, attempting to draw his red Ford Fiesta. "It's probably been impounded or something by now."

"Can it fly?" Teevar asked, resting his head on Mac's shoulder.

"Nah. It's not even that fast, to be honest." He drew a tree and a house and a dog outside on the lawn. Then he swiped the page and sketched another animal, squinting in concentration at the curly horns.

"Lenara?" Teevar asked.

Mac chuckled. "It's a goat," he said. "We use them for lots of things. Eating, milking, making clothes. Some people keep them as pets. Most people keep one of these." He drew another dog and then a cat by its side.

"I'd like to see Earth," Teevar said, his voice soft.

Mac kissed the top of his head. "You will," he said. "One day."

"I'm tired," Teevar said. "I think I do need to see a doctor."

"We'll find you a doctor." Mac put an arm around Teevar's shoulders. "Lenara's on it right now. It won't be long, I promise."

MAC HAD RETURNED to his own room eventually and slept fitfully, dreaming strange dreams of Earth and aliens and something about goats he couldn't quite remember. He rubbed his eyes and rolled over onto his back.

"*Psst.*"

He awoke with a start to find Ral peering over him, her face inches from his own. "What the hell?"

"You're naked," she said. "Put some clothes on, something bad's happened." She backed up and retreated out of the room.

Frowning, Mac dressed quickly and flung the door open. "What's going on?"

Ral didn't reply; she just set off down the corridor, glancing back over her shoulder to make sure he was following. She led him to the medical bay and waved him in first.

Mac stepped foot into the room, nervous of what to expect. He froze in the doorway when he saw Eesha. Blood covered the bed, the floor, and the kovan herself—she lay on the bed, still bound, and very, very still.

"Shit." Mac hurried to her, hesitated because of all the blood, and then tapped her cheek gently. "Eesha? Shit. Shit! Eesha, can you hear me?" With shaking hands, Mac felt for a pulse at her neck. He shook his head and looked back at Ral. "She's dead."

"Yes. I thought so." Ral bared her teeth in a grimace. "I wouldn't touch anything else, she might be contagious."

"It's what Teevar has," Mac explained, stepping back from the bed and staring wide-eyed at his bloody hands. "I don't know if other species can get it, or..." He shifted his gaze to Eesha's lifeless body. "She must've been prone to it or not as strong as Teevar or...I don't know. She didn't seem sick yesterday."

"Go and wash up," Ral said. "There's nothing we can do now. We've all been exposed. I will...I will dispose of the body."

Mac nodded. He didn't ask how Ral intended to do that—he supposed she'd flush the body into space. He squeezed past her and left the room, holding his hands out in front of him as if they were toxic.

Back in his room, Mac hurried into his shower cubicle and stood there, fully clothed, letting the water soak him. *He* didn't feel ill at all; he had no hint of a cough...did he? Was that a tickle at the back of his throat? He cleared his throat and shook his head at himself.

*Stop it.* He needed to talk to Lenara, check if they were any closer to getting help for Teevar. Seeing how quickly it had affected Eesha made him worry how long he had left. And *that* thought made him sick to his stomach. He shrugged his clothes off, turned off the water, and quickly dried himself before dashing out into the room and flinging his stuff everywhere in a bid to find clean clothes. Once he was dressed again, he practically ran from the room and made his way to Teevar's.

The door to Teevar's room was open, and Mac took just a two-second glance inside to see it was empty. He figured Teevar must be praying again, so hurried to the star room, trying to tamp down the fear.

Teevar turned and smiled at him as he entered. "I heard you coming. What's the panic?"

Mac relaxed and breathed an inward sigh of relief. He joined Teevar in the room. "Have you heard about Eesha?"

"Yes. I have asked the Gods to give her safe passage to the other side." Teevar turned and gazed out the far-side window, his hands neatly clasped behind his back.

Mac wondered how he could be so calm, what he was thinking. He didn't know what to say, or how to make Teevar feel better, so he said nothing.

"If I die—"

"Don't."

"*If* I die, please bury my body in the soil. I couldn't bear to be flushed into space; I need to be in the ground. I need to be part of something again."

"You're not going to die." Mac laughed a little, as if the suggestion was preposterous.

"Mackenzie." Teevar turned and lifted a hand to stroke Mac's cheek. "I'm fighting this. You need to be strong too, okay? I feel like, with you, I can beat anything."

Mac nodded. "You can." He took Teevar's hand. "We're totally gonna kick this illness's arse."

Teevar smiled. He kissed Mac and then turned to gaze at the stars once more.

# Chapter Nine

DAYS PASSED. TEEVAR didn't get any worse, but his condition didn't improve either. Mac lay awake some nights, listening to him cough. Sometimes when he woke after they'd shared a bed, there was blood on the pillow. It got to the stage where he'd go to ask Lenara if she'd found somewhere and she'd shake her head before he even opened his mouth.

He stood outside the cockpit, head pressed against the cool metal, the gentle vibration buzzing through his forehead, dreading that gesture. Eventually he took a deep breath and moved away from the wall.

"Mac?" Lenara called out before he entered, and he frowned.

"Yeah?"

"We are back on course. Tell Teevar. By the end of the day, we will be among civilisation."

Mac laughed. He stuck his head into the cockpit and grinned at Lenara when she turned to him. "You're bloody brilliant," he said. "I mean, it took you long enough, but you're bloody brilliant."

"Of course." Lenara smiled at him. "Tell Teevar."

"Right. Thanks!"

Mac stopped by the kitchen to grab a celebratory drink before he made his way to Teevar's room. He tapped on the door and entered with a wide smile. But it soon dropped when he saw Teevar sitting on the bed, holding a bloodied square of cloth to his nose.

"It won't stop," Teevar said, his voice muffled. "It won't stop bleeding."

Mac hurried to the bed, dumped the bottle on the floor, and put an arm around Teevar's waist. "It's okay. Head forwards. Pinch the bridge of your nose—that's it." His heart ached. "Lenara's found a planet. We'll be there in a few hours, right? So you just relax. Don't stress out or anything; that probably raises blood pressure or something. Just lie back and relax. Think calming thoughts—"

"Mac." Teevar moved the cloth from his face and a sluggish line of blood ran from his right nostril. He smiled. "We've found a planet! That's wonderful. Everything will be okay now." He held Mac's hand and gave it a squeeze. "Everything will be okay."

THE CHANGE IN pressure when they descended through the planet's atmosphere made Teevar vomit blood. When Lenara opened the doors after landing, the heat from the planet blasted inside as if they'd opened an oven. Mac, happy to let Lenara and Ral worry about the logistics of finding a doctor, stayed with Teevar inside the *Veena* and concentrated on trying to keep him cool.

It wasn't long before Teevar became unresponsive. Mac wrung out the cloth, changed the water again, and muttered expletives when it barely felt cool at all. He wet the cloth once more and placed it on Teevar's brow anyway.

"The girls will be back soon," he said. "Don't go anywhere. They're bringing that doctor back. Teevar? Don't make me talk to myself, eh? I sound like a crazy person. Teevar?"

The heat made sweat slide down Mac's back and his clothes cling to him. He wiped the back of his arm across his forehead and grimaced at the wetness.

"I could do with this," he joked, dabbing Teevar's brow again. "It's your turn to look after me next. That'll be nice, right? You can mop my brow and fan me. Maybe feed me some grapes, if you can find some."

He sighed. The paleness of Teevar's skin and the stillness of him was terrifying. "I've never worried about anybody this much before," he whispered. "I've not told you this but...I have nobody on Earth. Nobody to care about. Nobody who cares about me. You make me frightened and...*alive*. If you die." He cleared his throat and got to his feet. "Don't you bloody die. Teevar?"

"Mackenzie!"

The shout through Mac's comms made him rush from the room and down the stairs to the open door in the cargo bay. Ral and Lenara were riding a hover bike across the planet's dusty surface, kicking up a storm of sand around them. Both wore goggles and protective silver clothing they hadn't been wearing when they'd left. Mac realised a second bike was at their side, and the rider was much larger than the pair of them. He lifted his gaze and spotted buildings shimmering on the horizon.

The bikes stopped before the door, and Ral and Lenara dismounted and hurried to help the large rider from his bike. The creature was a hulking mass of dark flesh and muscle, and moved slowly up the gangway—the walk clearly an effort.

"This is Penvo," Lenara said, lifting her goggles as she helped him into the ship. "He's a doctor. He can help."

"Had to pay him," Ral added, standing the other side of Penvo as she too helped him aboard.

Penvo didn't appear to have much dexterity. He didn't even have a neck as far as Mac could tell. But his black lips smiled at Mac, and he felt a little better.

"He's worse," Mac said, walking ahead of Penvo, hoping to usher him on faster. "He's unconscious and too hot, but his skin feels cold. He's pale. And—"

Lenara put a hand on Mac's shoulder. "He is a good doctor. He will see."

Mac nodded. He entered Teevar's room first and crouched beside the bed. "Teevar, the doctor's here to see you. You'll be okay." He smoothed Teevar's hair from his forehead and then stepped back for the doctor. Ral and Lenara waited outside the room, and Mac glanced at them.

Penvo shuffled close to the bed. He held his hands palm down and ran them over Teevar's prone body, not touching him at all. He made a few grunts, took a step back, and then bent over at the waist to peer at Teevar's face. It sure as hell didn't look like any sort of doctor/patient examination Mac had ever seen before. He chewed his thumbnail and said nothing.

A thick, black tongue protruded from Penvo's mouth and lapped at the breath coming from Teevar's nostrils. He grunted again and straightened up.

"Bleeding," he said. His voice, like his movements, was laboured and slow.

"Yes, we know that," Mac said through gritted teeth. "Can't you make him better?"

Slowly, Penvo turned and faced him. He raised his left arm and moved his hand towards Mac's face. Mac backed up until he hit the wall and Penvo's large hand smothered him. He let out a muffled cry, and a sharp pain pierced his mind. When Penvo moved his hand away, Mac could taste blood on his lips.

"Different," Penvo said. "But enough of the same."

Mac dabbed at his lips and then frowned at his bloodied fingers. "You made me bleed!" he hissed. "What did you do? What the hell is going on?"

"Your blood," Penvo said. Then he pointed at Teevar.

"What?" Mac growled in irritation and looked towards Ral and Lenara. "One of you better know what the *hell* he's talking about—"

"Teevar needs your blood," Lenara said.

Mac blinked. *A transfusion?*

"Yes." Penvo ambled to the door and touched Ral on the shoulder. "My bag," he said. "Please." Then to Lenara, he said, "Your medical facility."

Lenara nodded and looked to Mac. "We'll move Teevar into the medical bay. Help me lift him."

Mac stirred himself into action. He squeezed past Penvo and carefully took hold of Teevar under the arms as Lenara took his feet. He didn't say a word as they carried him out of the room and down to the medical bay, where they laid him on the bed.

"Are you all right?" Lenara asked.

"Hm? Oh." Mac rubbed his face and pulled his gaze from Teevar. "I guess so."

Lenara glanced back to make sure they were alone, then she placed her hands on Mac's shoulders. "I do not know if this will work. I do not know if this is safe. I do know that you don't have to do this."

Mac laughed though it sounded hollow. "I *have* to do this."

Lenara nodded. "Then be strong."

She left the room, whether to help Penvo, find Ral, or give him some privacy, he didn't know. He turned to Teevar and touched his face. "I don't really know what's going on," he admitted. "Or how it came to this. But I think we're going to use my blood to make you better. We do this on Earth... I've never given blood though. I should've done. I should've done a lot of things. I should've been nicer or, I don't know, given money to charity or something. This is probably some sort of shitty karma thing. If there is a god, or...*gods*, I hope they're watching over us now. I hope—"

He stopped when he heard footsteps outside the room and cleared his throat. Penvo shuffled into the room, Lenara and Ral—with his bag—just behind him.

"What do I need to do?" Mac asked, hovering about near the bed. "I mean, do I need to scrub up or anything?"

"Sit," Penvo said. "Sit."

Mac pulled a chair close to the bed and sat. Penvo worked around him, instructing Lenara and Ral, but Mac could only stare at Teevar, his heart leaping into his throat every time he thought the kovan's chest had stopped rising and falling.

He swallowed and shifted his gaze to Penvo as the being took hold of his arm and slid a needle into his skin. It barely hurt at all. Blood flowed into a clear tube and down into where Penvo had inserted the other end into Teevar's arm. Mac didn't know how long he had to sit like that for. Penvo gestured for him to open and close his fist, so he did that, supposing it was meant to keep the blood flowing.

Lenara and Ral hung around for a while until they disappeared only for Lenara to return a few moments later with food—which Mac waved away until Penvo encouraged him to eat. Then she disappeared again. Penvo ate and then stayed in the room, silent and unmoving. Mac stared at Teevar until his eyelids drooped.

*It's not as hot*, he thought. And he fell asleep.

MAC WOKE TO somebody calling his name. He opened his eyes, but his vision was hazy and strange, as if he was still in a dream.

"Mackenzie?" Teevar leant over him. "Mac?"

Mac blinked. He moved his arms, but they were too heavy; his lips wouldn't form words properly either, and his tongue felt fat and dry. He sighed and fell into sleep again.

When he next woke, he could sit up, though his head spun. He realised he was still in the medical bay, and he spotted Teevar asleep on the bed where he'd left him. The tube no longer connected them, and Penvo had vacated the room. Mac swung his legs over the bed, wondering if Penvo had laid him there, or if the girls had moved him, and walked over to Teevar, his legs shaky at first until he woke up a little more.

He couldn't tell if Teevar had more colour in his cheeks or if it was his imagination. He took hold of Teevar's hand, feeling how clammy his skin was. The air seemed cooler in the medical bay, and when Mac stopped to pay attention, he heard *Veena's* engines and figured the ship had some sort of air conditioning or climate control or...something.

His arm was sore where the needle had pierced his skin, and he eyed the bruise he'd gained. Stifling a yawn, he let go of Teevar's hand long enough to press his comms. "Lenara? Ral?"

"You are awake," Lenara replied. "How do you feel?"

"Knackered."

There was a pause. Unsure if that had translated, Mac added, "Tired."

"How is Teevar?"

"Asleep. I think he looks better. I think I might've spoken to him earlier." He rubbed his forehead. "Are we flying?"

"No. Penvo would like to check on you both again before he leaves."

Mac nodded, though Lenara couldn't see him. He turned as somebody else entered the medical bay and relaxed when he saw it was Ral. She approached the bed and sniffed the air around Teevar.

"He smells better. Less like death."

"He looks better," Mac agreed, turning back to the bed.

Ral placed a tray of food on the side. "For you both. Penvo said you both needed to eat to keep your strength up now." Her ears twitched, and she sidled up to the bed. "I'm pleased you're both still alive."

"Thanks." Mac smiled. "My face might not show it, but I'm bloody ecstatic."

"We are all pleased." They turned to see Lenara standing in the doorway. She gave Mac a grateful nod of her head.

"Yeah. Well, we have to see if Teevar wakes up next." His stomach rumbled, and he reached over for the food Ral had brought. The lupa squeezed past Lenara and quietly left the room.

Mac chewed the food and tried to concentrate on the taste rather than think about what exactly his blood had done for Teevar. Had it cured him? Or just kept him stable for now? He'd have to ask Penvo. He swallowed and reached for another piece.

Lenara joined him in gazing at Teevar. "He looks peaceful."

"He's still, right?" He'd tried not to let the worry creep into his voice, but even he could hear the tremble. Lenara placed her hand on his shoulder.

"He is. But he is not convulsing or vomiting or bleeding. That is down to you." She reached over and touched the top of Teevar's head ever so gently before she pulled back and turned away. "Do not hesitate to call if you need me."

Mac nodded. After Lenara left, he wondered if she meant within the next few hours or if her offer had no expiry. He rubbed his eyes and turned for more food.

"Mac?"

Mac almost choked on his mouthful as he hurried to Teevar's bedside. "I'm here. You're awake!"

Teevar smiled sleepily up at him. "I met the doctor," he murmured. "I have your blood. We share the same blood."

"We do now. You're part human, eh?" He held Teevar's hand as the other man reached out for him. "Are you okay? Do you feel okay?"

Teevar sighed deeply. "Penvo said...he said your blood...it healed me."

"Oh thank god." Mac pressed a kiss to Teevar's forehead. "I was *so* worried."

"I'm fine." Teevar lifted a hand to Mac's cheek. "Thank you," he said. "Thank you."

"Anytime." Mac gazed into Teevar's blue eyes before planting a tender kiss on his lips. "I love you." He pulled back, but Teevar was asleep once more.

# Chapter Ten

"So, everything's fine, right?" Mac asked, watching as Penvo ran his palms over Teevar. "Right? He's properly fixed? Cured?"

"Cured," Penvo confirmed, slowly lowering his arms. "Miracle."

"Really?" Mac flashed Teevar a grin. "Those gods of yours are watching over you."

Penvo moved to pick up his bag, but Mac snatched it up before he could reach it and handed it over. "You'll be heading home now?"

"Yes," Penvo agreed. "Home."

"Not a big talker," Mac said. He winked at Teevar and then ushered Penvo from the room and out to where Ral and Lenara were waiting. "We've got the all clear," he said. "You can take the doc home."

"We will be leaving as soon as we return," Lenara said, heading down the stairs before Penvo and turning back to watch he came down safely with Ral taking up the rear. "Keep the engine running. I cannot return to the heat."

"Got it, boss." Mac waited until he'd seen them leave before he returned to Teevar in the medical bay. He was surprised to see him standing. "Should you be up?"

"I'm hungry." Teevar selected a piece of food from the tray. "And I'm sick of lying down."

Mac joined him and slipped an arm around his waist. "I'll fetch us something fresh."

"Mac? I'm sick of running."

Mac turned back. "We're not going to get caught, and we don't have the money to pay the bounty hunters anymore. We have to keep run—" He looked at Teevar. "My pin. I dropped it when the kovans first took me. If I could get it back, it could get us to Earth. I know it could."

Teevar smiled. "Then we go and get your pin."

"That easy?"

"I will take my chance with anything after what I've been through."

Mac nodded. "You can help me convince Lenara then." He grinned and then left to get them some more food.


"Cernod," Lenara said.

Mac looked up from the star charts spread out over the table in the kitchen. "What?"

"The planet where we found you." Lenara tapped one of the charts. "Cernod."

"Right." Mac frowned over the charts and pretended he could understand all the marks and squiggles. Teevar and Ral sat opposite him and Lenara, Teevar looking brighter than he had in days while Ral looked fed up. The lupa rested her chin on her hands on top of the table and let out a huff.

"What is the matter?" Lenara asked.

"Earth," Ral said. "Teevar might fit in there, but how will I? How will you? Why do we have to go to Mac's home world? Why not mine?"

"You don't have to come with us," Mac said. "But if you want to stay hidden, then Earth's a good place to hide. You'll fit in just fine!" He didn't believe that, of course. He suspected Ral and Lenara would be carted away and experimented on—Teevar too, if they didn't believe he was human. Mac would have to keep them out of sight, that was all; maybe make a few friends in high places and then introduce the aliens slowly and take it from there. Or perhaps he could move to somewhere remote. Or....

"Isn't there some sort of technology that can make you look like something else?" he asked. "A what's it called—a glamour. Or, I don't know. Plastic surgery?"

Ral snorted. "Magic. I don't want to look like you. You look like pink hinkle worms."

"And smell like an oosh dog," Lenara added. "I am not sure we can replicate the smell."

Mac frowned. "Hey, do I insult you people? No, I don't. Neither of you can come to Earth. I retract my invitation." He glared at them and then stomped out of the room, not looking back when he heard Teevar run after him.

"They're nervous," Teevar said, catching up with him. "Your planet has had no contact with alien lifeforms before. You don't know how your people will react any more than we do."

Mac dragged a hand through his hair. "No, I don't," he agreed. "And I don't want them to come if it'll put them in danger. You said you didn't want to run anymore, and I don't know a better hiding place than Earth." He sighed and sank down to the floor before drawing his knees up to rest his elbows on them. He held his head in his hands.

Teevar sat by his side. "Perhaps we should've stayed on Penvo's planet."

"That place was hotter than hell. Probably would've all died from heat exhaustion or something. We should find another planet and settle there—I don't think the bounty hunters have any idea where we are. Bloody hell, I've not even seen any in all the time I've been here."

Teevar rested his head on Mac's shoulder. "You're lucky you've not seen them. They frighten me."

A loud clang rocked the whole ship, reverberating through the hull and knocking Mac and Teevar over. Mac was just scrambling to his feet when Lenara ran from the kitchen and thundered past him.

"What's going on?" Mac called.

"They've got us," Lenara replied, not turning back. "They've got us!"

"What the fuck...?" Mac took Teevar's hands and pulled him to his feet. Then he ran after Lenara. He burst into the cockpit after her and gaped when he saw the view out the window.

A large ship, easily three times the size of the *Veena*, flew directly in front of them. The ship was black and angular and reminded him a little of a Ford Cadillac without the wheels. Something long and snake-like had attached itself to Lenara's ship, and she was smacking buttons and swiping consoles to find out where.

"I am reversing," she said. "But they are reeling us in like giberl fish."

"Who the hell are they?"

"The bounty hunters."

Mac turned to see Teevar behind him, with Ral standing just in the doorway. Teevar's blue eyes were wide.

"Well, can't we get free?" Mac asked. "Can't we break free somehow?"

"I am trying!" Lenara yanked the controls, but the *Veena* jerked like a deer in a bear trap. "They have their hooks in us," she said, pulling up one of the images on the console and making it larger. It showed the

*Veena* and a red flashing light blinking just under the right engine. "I can lose this panel here, flush it, but we will lose some stability."

"Won't that open us up to space?" Mac asked. "Won't we all get sucked out into oblivion?" The bounty hunters' ship grew ever larger as it drew nearer, and Mac grit his teeth, his whole body taut.

"Not if we seal this room off." Teevar squeezed past Mac to tap a point on the console. "Seal this and the rest of the ship is safe. I don't know how long the internal door can hold though, but..."

A look passed between him and Lenara. Before Mac could argue further, Lenara slammed a button. The ship rocked and then, through the window, he could see the rope slacken and a green panel from *Veena's* hull float past.

"Please tell me you sealed us off first?" Mac asked. "Jesus bleeding Christ."

The *Veena* turned and the black ship disappeared out of their view. With a determined look on her face, Lenara said, "Brace for FTL."

"Oh fu—"

Mac only had time to grab the back of Lenara's chair before everything went dark. He hadn't meant to hold his breath—didn't even know if he'd made that action himself, or if the speed they were travelling had knocked the air out of him—but his ears popped and he let out a breath just as the lights came back on.

He could see planets, two of them, outside the window. One was blue and green and had an atmosphere filled with clouds; the other was smaller and a dull red. For a moment, he thought he was looking at Earth.

"Mod," Ral said, pointing a clawed hand past Mac's face to the red planet. "And his sister, Iona-Ra."

"Is that where you're from?" Mac asked, remembering she was from the same planet as the skreens.

Ral shook her head. "It is controlled by the skreens, though. I have been there maybe five times." She grinned, showing her pointed teeth. "You will be safe with me."

"We have no choice but to land," Lenara said. "Safe or not. If we stay up here much longer, our hull will breach. I am taking us down. Ral, sit. Guide me."

Mac moved out of the way so that Ral could help Lenara. He left the cockpit with Teevar and they stood just outside. His skin tingled as the adrenaline faded away.

Teevar smiled. "And you stay lucky, Mackenzie Jones. You've still not seen the hunters."

"Think I've seen enough," Mac said. "Remind me to show you a Ford Cadillac when we get to Earth."

THE WIND WHIPPED up outside the ship, making dry leaves skitter against *Veena's* metal shell. Ral advised them to wrap up, so Mac spent some time sorting his outfit and wondering if he'd look an idiot if he wrapped a scarf around his head or if it'd be stylish on this planet. In the end he opted to just wrap it around the lower part of his face and joined the others to leave the ship.

When the door opened, they were faced with nothing but a great expanse of water.

"Great," Mac said. "Where's this city? Can't exactly pick up any ship parts around here, can we? I thought you knew this place, Ral?"

Ral picked up a stone, showed Mac her teeth, and then threw it towards the water. The stone struck something solid—a city shimmered into view and then vanished again.

"Easy if you know how," she said. She stepped out onto the water and carried on walking, soon disappearing from sight.

Mac and the others followed her, and the city sprang into life as soon as they passed through the barrier. Except it was like no city Mac had ever seen before. The buildings looked as if they'd been carved from mountains, and they were set in neat blocks just as if somebody had built them up from a Lego set. The denizens of the city were insectoid—some with iridescent wings, all with multiple limbs. They wore clothes, which was weird, but Mac was pleased he didn't have to look at naked insect parts, and the fact that they took barely any notice of them at all meant they were obviously used to off-worlders.

"Do you know where we can buy what we need for *Veena*?" Lenara asked.

"No," Ral said. "But there will be somewhere. Keep your eyes open."

"These...bug people," Mac said, "do they speak our language?"

"Why don't you ask one," Ral suggested.

That felt like a dare to Mac, so he stopped one of the bug people. It towered over him, but leaned down a little to hear what he had to say. "Excuse me, do you know where we can find a mechanic?"

Mandibles clicked and antennae quivered. Mac didn't think he'd get an answer. Then the bug said, "Head two blocks down and turn left. On the right, there is a workshop run by kovans. Ask for Gesak Gol Minsak. He will give you a discount if you say Merskip sent you."

Mac raised his eyebrows. "Bloody brilliant. Cheers!"

Merskip waved his antennae and then turned and continued on his way. Mac grinned at the gang. "I like this planet already," he said. "You heard the man! Two blocks down and left."

"That was a female," Ral said, passing him.

"Ah." Mac shrugged. He winked at Teevar and then set off after Ral. The wind whistled down the street, lifting dust into the air, so Mac lifted his scarf over his nose. All the insect people seemed to be walking in the same direction, he noticed, the only ones walking against the flow were his group and other non-natives. He wondered where they were all going.

It didn't take long to reach the workshop. The building looked the same as all the others: grey, square, rock. A sign showing something that resembled a hammer hung over the door. Mac glanced at the building next door to see a similar sign hanging there, although it showed a symbol he didn't recognise.

Teevar opened the door and headed inside and Mac and the girls followed. It was brighter than Mac envisaged and appeared clean and modern. A kovan man who'd been poring over a complex-looking system of cogs and gears stopped what he was doing to welcome them.

He plastered a smile on his face as he approached. "Greetings," he said. "Welcome—" his gaze flicked to the gold pendant around Teevar's neck, "—*Pryster*. How can I be of service?" He touched index fingers with Teevar, Mac, Lenara, and then finally, Ral.

"Pryster Teevar Nok Dimar," Teevar said. "I'd like to speak to Gesak Gol Minsak, if possible."

"You are speaking to him." Gesak gave a short bow and smiled again.

"Merskip sent us," Mac said, keen to get that in quickly. "She was singing your praises, said you're the best there is."

"A loyal customer. What can I do for you today?"

Lenara stepped forwards. "My ship needs some work. A new panel to repair damage to the hull."

"My team and I can do that for you, no problem. It would be fifteen-hundred boule if you wanted the work done today."

"Fifteen hundred?" Mac repeated. "What if we wanted it done tomorrow?" He shook his head. "Merskip assured us you lot weren't rip-off merchants, she said 'That Gesak, he's a right decent bloke, very trustworthy.' Didn't she say that, Teevar?"

Teevar raised his eyebrows. "Um. Yes. Exactly that." He cleared his throat. "If we could agree on a thousand boule, I would perform a blessing for you and ask the gods to favour your business with prosperity."

Gesak at least had the decency to look as if he was considering the offer before he said, "Twelve hundred."

Teevar looked to Mac for help, so Mac sighed sadly and shook his head. "The gods would be most disappointed you weren't willing to show generosity towards one of their representatives. Come on, guys. I think we need to look elsewhere."

"Wait!" Gesak said. "For you, eleven hundred. And Pryster, if you could extend your blessings upon my household..."

"Of course," Teevar agreed. He held out his index finger and touched it to Gesak's. "We have an agreement."

Mac rubbed his hands together. "Great. Where do we sign?"

As the ship belonged to Lenara, and Teevar had made the deal, Gesak took them both aside to finalise the agreement and hand over the money, leaving Ral and Mac to nose around the workshop. They stopped in front of the machine Gesak had been working on when they entered, and Ral swished her tail like a cat on the hunt.

"Do you know what that is?" she asked.

"Not a bloody clue," Mac said.

"They use these in the bank to control the doors. Cogs turn, click, click, click, and the doors lock down."

Mac eyed the machine. "Looks kinda easy to break, right?" he commented. "If you jammed the gears, the doors would stay open."

"Designed not to jam," Ral said. "And they're encased in stone once in position so nobody can tamper with them."

"Uh huh. What if somebody, hypothetically, tampered with it now?"

"They probably test it before installation."

"And, hypothetically, what would happen if somebody managed to tamper with it after it'd already been tested?"

Ral flashed him her white teeth. "A person wishing to tamper with it would need to hang around," she said. "And then they would need to find out when it was being installed, and they would have to be at the bank ready to take advantage of the jam because it would not happen again. If somebody did manage to tamper with it, they could rob the bank."

Mac glanced at Ral. "We're hanging around, right?"

"Absolutely." Ral turned and smiled as Teevar, Lenara, and Gesak joined them once again.

"They're going to start work right away," Teevar said. "Lenara will take Gesak and his team to the ship, and I will perform a blessing. You two—"

"We're going to get some air," Mac said. "Maybe grab a bite to eat. We'll pick up something for you guys. Catch you later."

Before Teevar could quiz him, Mac headed for the door, looking back at Ral to follow him. She took the hint and joined him outside.

"Where's the bank?" he asked. "If you're thinking what I'm thinking, then we need to plan this. And we'll need to get Teevar and Lenara on board too. It seems too easy. Why was nobody guarding that machine?"

"It's not finished," Ral said. "And you haven't seen who guards the bank. Come on."

They walked down the street together—pausing to pick up food from a street vendor when Ral's nose led them off course—before they stopped outside yet another nondescript grey building. This one had a sign hanging outside which quite clearly showed a pile of boule.

"In we go." Mac opened the door and held it for Ral. After what she'd said, he wasn't surprised to see skreens inside, several armed with large guns. The ceiling was high and the room large and echoey. A long desk, with four of the insectoids serving customers, lay at the back of the room, at either side of which were two more doors leading into the rest of the bank.

"Have you got anything to deposit?" Mac asked. "I have nothing."

"We have to deposit something?"

"I want to see how this place works."

Ral reached into her pocket and brought out a familiar-looking spiky glass paperweight. Mac's eyes widened as it dawned on him where he'd seen it before, and he laughed. "You stole that from Kelrar!" he hissed. "Didn't he say it was dangerous?"

"If it blows up the bank then it will help us," Ral said, shrugging. She went to the desk when one of the servers became free of customers and put the paperweight on the top of it. "I wish to make a deposit."

Mac stood by her side. He quickly reached out and stopped the server from touching the glass.

"Careful," he warned. "This thing is worth a fortune. We'd like to see your vaults before we store it with you. We need somewhere secure."

Ral took the paperweight and pocketed it again as the server rounded the desk. She bared her teeth at a skreen as they passed by, but the creature, luckily, didn't notice. Mac tried to take in every detail as they followed the insectoid through a second set of doors, but the place was devoid of much personality and had little to look at.

"If somebody was to break in," Mac said, "how could we be sure they wouldn't make off with our goods?"

"The doors come down, sir," the insect said, as if he'd asked a stupid question. "The vaults lock. Nobody would get past the skreens. Your deposit is safe with us."

They wandered through another open doorway into a circular room that had many small doors covering all the walls. The insect walked to one of them and pressed a button to open it up. "You place your deposit in here, and it will stay here, secure, until you come to collect it again."

"I take it this place goes into lockdown at night," Mac said. "I mean, the doors don't stay open all the time."

The insect's antennae quivered. "We lockdown before we leave, yes."

Ral pushed a button on another of the deposit boxes but it didn't open. "These are locked," she said.

"Only we jokats are able to open them. The buttons are controlled by sensors set to our exoskeletons. They do not react to skin or hair or fur."

"So one of you guys could rob the place," Mac said, wondering how on earth they could get one of the insectoids to open the boxes for them to steal the money.

"Jokats don't steal, Mac," Ral said. "I think our deposit will be safe here." She withdrew the paperweight from her pocket again and placed it into the open deposit box, standing back to let the jokat close it up.

They returned to the desk once more, and Ral handed over boule for the payment of their deposit. Once they left the building, Mac said, "Doable?"

"I think so," Ral said.

"I do too. We tamper with the cogs after testing and then make sure we're ready at lockdown on the day it's being installed. I presume the skreens guard at night but...we can take them, right? I'm a pretty good shot, as is Lenara. Four guns between us? It's just getting those boxes open and making sure we're inside before lockdown."

"Let me worry about that," Ral said. "You work on convincing the others."

"All right," Mac said. "It's a deal."

# Chapter Eleven

THEY SAT IN the *Veena's* kitchen, quietly munching on the food they'd bought from the city. Mac tried to gauge Teevar's reaction and couldn't. Lenara ground nuts between her teeth.

"So," she said, "when exactly are you expecting to put this plan into action?"

"After they've run the final testing for the machine that controls the doors," Mac answered. "Leave that to me. I'll do some digging. How long before Gesak finishes fixing the hull?"

"Three days. Perhaps longer."

Mac looked to Teevar. "What do you think?"

"We could do with the money," Teevar conceded. "But I'm not happy with theft."

"We'll only take what we need." Mac reached across the table and gave Teevar's hand a squeeze. "If you don't want to do it, we'll forget all about it."

Teevar closed his eyes. He was silent for a moment or two, asking his gods or searching his conscience—Mac wasn't really sure—but eventually he opened his eyes and gave Mac a nod. "No," he said. "No, let's do it."

Mac grinned. "Yeah? Brilliant." He tucked into his food, excited at the prospect of pulling off a bank job.

After they'd eaten, Mac and Teevar walked into the city together, enjoying time alone while Ral and Lenara stayed back to watch Gesak's team measuring up for the new panel.

"Show me this bank," Teevar said, and Mac walked with him down the street to the bank, and they stood and gazed at it from the other side of the street. Mac folded his arms, waiting for some sort of reaction from Teevar.

A group of jokats walked by them, obscuring their view.

"I hope your plan works."

"Come on," Mac said. "I'm lucky, remember?"

Teevar smiled. "You're a bad influence," he said. He walked on again, and the pair of them spent the next few hours exploring the city. Mac bought more clothes and was almost tempted by a small furry creature in a cage until it bit his finger. The shopkeeper waved them away, and the pair of them burst into laughter when they got outside.

"Did you have pets on Earth, Mac?" Teevar asked.

"Nah. Don't think I should be trusted to look after anything other than myself. Did you have any animals?"

Teevar shook his head. "No pets allowed at the temple. But we did keep fish for eating."

"And what about family?"

Teevar smiled a little. "My parents died when I was very young. My brothers and sisters at the temple were my family. I must admit, I miss them terribly."

"I haven't got a family either," Mac said. "So nobody's missing me."

"Really?" Teevar held Mac's hand briefly, still shy of showing affection in public. "No friends?"

Mac shrugged. "Doesn't bother me. Anyway, this is depressing talk. Let's do something else."

"And what would you suggest?"

"I was going to suggest trying on all my new clothes and seeing how handsome I looked." Mac hoisted his bag of goodies up onto his shoulder. "But seeing the look in your eye, I think you have other ideas I'll probably like better."

"Yes," Teevar agreed, smiling. "I think I do."


MAC PEERED AT the cogs and gears as one of Gesak's assistants, who was wearing a massive eyeglass, concentrated on fitting another piece to the machine.

"Don't touch anything," he warned. "Please step back."

Mac held up his hands. "I just find it fascinating," he said. "You're not looking for an apprentice, are you? I'm sure I could do this work."

The man sat back from his work and lifted the eyeglass so he could eyeball Mac instead. "No. Please go away. This is *highly* skilled *important* work."

"All right. I'll go." Mac backed away. "But can I see it in action? Please? It's amazing, a credit to you. It would mean everything to me if I could see it. From a distance, even. I could watch it from a distance, and I would die happy. I—"

"Fine! I will find you when it's ready to be tested and you can watch it then. From a distance."

The man scowled at him so Mac gave him a grin. "Thank you. You've made my day."

He turned and left the workshop. His heart thumped enough for him to be aware of it, but it was a nervous excitement and made him feel good to be alive.

The next day, however, the nerves really kicked in, and Teevar came across him throwing up in the bushes behind where Lenara had parked the *Veena.*

"It's happening," Mac explained, as Teevar rubbed his back, staring wide-eyed at the steam coming off his vomit. "It's happening. Tomorrow. Tell the others. Tell Ral to do whatever it is she needs to do. It's happening tomorrow."

In the morning, Mac and the others ate breakfast together. They watched as Gesak and his team sealed the last part of the panel to *Veena's* hull and briefly discussed extra payment if Lenara wanted the panel painted to match the rest of the ship. Then they returned to the workshop in the city, where Gesak sent out another of his staff to finalise the work and Lenara passed over a final payment.

Mac stood, bored, as money exchanged hands. He happened to glance over his shoulder and noticed the assistant standing over the machine—which was working. Frowning, he headed over.

"You promised me I could watch!"

"I did, and you can come back later," the man said. "This isn't the final test, it's not running smoothly. If you want to see it at its best, then come back later."

"I will," Mac said, turning away. "Don't forget." He took a deep breath to settle his nerves and offered Teevar a reassuring smile when he received a questioning look.

*Everything will go to plan*, he told himself. *Relax.*

They headed into the city, and Ral disappeared for a time, not telling anybody where she was going or what she was doing. Lenara also left them, though she soon returned with a gun for Teevar and another bigger one for herself.

As the sky began to darken over the city, Ral finally returned and they all ventured back into the workshop. Gesak met with them and informed them the work on *Veena* was complete. They thanked him, and Teevar promised him all the gods' blessings. The assistant came over and showed them the final test of the machine that would control the bank's doors. They made appropriate noises to show how impressed they were and that was that.

Just before they left, Ral chewed off one of her nails and spat it into the machine, where it lodged itself between the gears. Mac smiled and said nothing.

Outside, fire lanterns lit the streets in a flickering orange glow. The jokats, for the most part, seemed to have retired for the night, and the only people around were off-worlders.

"The bank closes shortly," Ral said. "They will install the new equipment as quickly as possible, ready for lockdown. We need to be there."

"Okay," Mac agreed. "I think we need to go and collect that paperweight of yours."

The four of them walked to the bank together and strolled inside, paying no attention to the members of Gesak's workforce they spotted. Mac approached the desk and smiled at the server. "We need to pick up our deposit."

"Box 5717," Ral added, fishing about in her pocket for the receipt she'd been given.

The jokat led them through the bank to the vault room, informing them the bank would be closing shortly and apologising for asking them to hurry along. When it opened the box for them, Mac was surprised to see two slabs of gold boule instead.

Ral thanked the jokat and took the money. She flashed Mac her teeth as if she knew something he didn't.

From outside, there came a deafening explosion and the building shook, sending rock dust floating down from above. There were cries from outside the room, and the sound of people running.

"What the hell?" Mac cried.

"Somebody's trying to break in," Ral said. Then to the jokat, "Do something!"

The jokat's mandibles clacked together and its antennae turned about as if it were nervous. "Lockdown is scheduled, but I can set it off before then. They won't get in. We need to get out. Quickly!"

Ral moved, she grabbed the jokat and smacked it hard between its head and its thorax, sending it crumbling to the floor in a heap.

Teevar gasped. "Have you killed it?"

"Unconscious. Help me!" Ral dragged the jokat to the boxes and began using its hand to unlock as many boxes as she could.

"What the hell was that explosion?" Mac asked, jogging to the door to peer out into the corridor. There was a grinding sound, and the door began to descend, shaking loose rock from the ceiling, before it came to a screeching halt.

"My paperweight," Ral said. "Blew the front door out. Nothing major, just a distraction. Switched deposits earlier."

"You're a bloody genius," Mac said, joining Ral and Teevar in emptying the boxes into their bags. Lenara stood guard at the door, her gun at the ready.

"Skreens are coming," she called. "Hurry!"

Above her, the door groaned, loud enough to make Mac look up just in time to yell, "Lenara, move!" before it came crashing down and sealed them in.

"Shit," Mac cursed as the dust cleared. "Shit! Now what?"

"We're trapped," Teevar said, his knuckles white from where he gripped his bag so hard. "It's the end. They'll catch us."

"Do not panic so." Lenara shouldered her gun and marched up to Teevar. She tied the handles of his bag around his neck and shoulders and pushed his gun into his hand. Taking the hint, Mac and Ral also carried their bags on their backs and Mac drew his weapon.

"We just shoot our way out?" he asked. "When will the doors come up?"

"I do not know," Lenara replied.

"Bloody fantastic. The doors were meant to jam," Mac said, rounding on Ral.

"They did jam," she snapped back at him.

"Not for long enough!"

The room was plunged into darkness and Mac froze, blinking into the black. His heart pounded so hard he wondered if anybody else could hear it. His eyes adjusted just enough for him to make out the shapes of the others.

"What's going on?" he hissed. "Are they trying to freak us out?"

"Looks that way," Teevar said. "How's your night vision?"

"Nonexistent," Mac said. "You have night vision?"

"Some."

"I can barely bloody see anything!" Mac said. "Ral? Lenara?"

"I can see fine," Ral said, her voice somewhere to the right of him.

"I can see well enough," Lenara said. "I can hear them behind the door. They don't sound many. We can still shoot our way out."

*We'll still be outnumbered.* There was a scuffle and a groan in the room; Mac realised the jokat was waking. Suddenly a hand clasped his ankle, and he cried out, kicking the jokat before he realised what he was doing. "Shit! Sorry! Shitting hell. Have I killed it? I think I've killed it!"

He could just make out Teevar by his side, moving to check on the jokat. "Alive. Help me sit him up."

Mac grabbed what he hoped was an arm and helped Teevar move the jokat to the back of the room and lean him up against the wall out the way. "He should be safe here," Teevar said, his voice quiet. "If they start shooting as soon as they bring the doors up, he should be safe."

"Are they likely to do that?" Mac asked.

Teevar didn't have a chance to answer as Lenara called out, "There are more of them arriving."

"Teevar," Mac said, reaching for him when he saw him move away. "If we die, at least I get to die with you by my side."

Teevar took hold of Mac's hands and then let them go to brush his fingers gently against Mac's cheek. "We'll not die. With your luck and the gods on our side, we can't lose."

Mac chuckled. "I think I'm going to rely more on Lenara's massive gun."

"That too." Teevar kissed Mac's lips and then his forehead as the sound of the doors grinding filled the room.

"Get ready," Lenara called.

Mac and Teevar joined Lenara and Ral in front of the door, the four of them standing side by side, ready to face whatever waited for them. Mac drew his weapon and held it with both hands, willing himself to stop shaking and *focus*.

The doors lifted up and up. They were barely head height when Ral said, "I'm going," and leapt under the doors and out into the room beyond.

"Ral!" Teevar yelled.

Shouts. Shooting. The doors continued to rise and the skreens appeared, just dark shapes in the gloom, lit in flashes from the gunshots. Mac fired, eyes wide. He strode forward with Teevar and Lenara and then dived to the side as a shot whizzed past his head.

He could make out Ral, practically leaping off the walls, causing confusion as she leapt onto skreen backs and bit into their necks. Lenara's weapon blasted out pulse shots with a *voom, voom,* and she grunted as a shot hit her in the shoulder but kept firing.

Mac ducked into a doorway, peeked out, and fired again. "Teevar?" he called.

The kovan thumped against the wall as he joined Mac. "Here," he said. "You okay?"

Mac nodded. "You?"

"Yes. Ready?"

Mac and Teevar emerged into the hallway again, firing shots at the skreens. The lights emitted from the shots streaked the air and the flashes burned into Mac's retinas. He could smell smoke and the hot-dry stink of the skreens. A body fell across the way and he stumbled over it before he could stop himself, landing heavily on his right shoulder. He grimaced, and then somebody was hauling him to his feet—Lenara—and he snatched up his gun and fired again.

Adrenaline narrowed his vision, sharpened it, and seemed to slow the world down. His eyes adjusted better to the low light than he'd imagined they could—unless of course the daylight was returning—and he saw skreens fall before him.

They were almost at the front door now, so close he could see rubble from Ral's explosion and the street beyond. A skreen loomed in front of him, too close for him to take a shot, and lights flashed in its eyes.

Then blood exploded at its temple, and it fell to the side. Mac looked over to see Teevar, one hand on his gun, the other clutching his gold pendant.

There was no time to do anything else but push on towards the door, and they were almost there, climbing over rubble, close...

"STOP!"

Mac turned at the shout. Teevar was by his side, Lenara somewhere just behind to the right. Ral was taken, held between two of the skreens, her arms pulled back behind her, blood dripping from her muzzle and her eyes fierce.

"We have your friend," the largest skreen said, stepping forwards. "Drop your weapons."

Mac hesitated and Teevar lowered his gun a little. Lenara backed up until she was beside them both but kept her gun trained on the skreens.

"Run, you idiots," Ral snapped. And she wrenched one of her arms free and sank her teeth into the skreen's hand.

Mac didn't see what happened next. Lenara grabbed both him and Teevar and dragged them on amid the shouts, pulling them from the building and out into the streets where they didn't need any more convincing to run.

For a while, footsteps followed them, but they didn't look back. They ran on, taking as many twists and turns as they could, until the three of them emerged from the city, puffing and out of breath.

Mac's muscles burned and the bag handles cut into his shoulders. He dumped the bag on the ground and practically dragged it to the *Veena*.

"What about Ral?" Teevar asked, glancing nervously back towards the water. "We can't leave her."

"She's probably dead, right?" Mac said. "They'd have killed her!"

Lenara opened up the ship and started up the gangway. "They won't kill her," she said. "They'll use her as bait to draw us out of hiding."

The door closed behind Mac and the lights came on inside, making him squint. The three of them trudged up the stairs, leaving their haul down in the cargo bay.

"We need to get off planet," Lenara said. "Teevar, fix my arm." She carried on to the cockpit and Teevar hurried off to the medical bay.

*Bloody hell*, Mac thought. His shoulder throbbed from where he'd fallen on it and vague thoughts of the ugly bruise he'd get circled at the back of his mind. *We can't leave Ral.* She'd sacrificed herself for them. If the skreens were keeping her alive, they needed to get her back.

The *Veena* rumbled to life, and he knew they were heading for space. He made his way to the cockpit, where Teevar was concentrating on sealing Lenara's wound.

"We have to go back for her," Mac said.

"They'll be looking for us," Lenara said. "They'll be ready for us as soon as we land."

"We *have* to go back."

Lenara winced, and Teevar moved away from her. "We will," she said. "But we need a plan first."

# Chapter Twelve

MAC AND TEEVAR fell into bed together, too tired to even change their clothes, and slept curled up in each other's arms. Mac woke once to Teevar sitting on the edge of the bed, muttering softly to his pendant in the half-light.

"For Ral?" he murmured.

"Yes."

Mac sat up and put his arms around Teevar. "She's tough," he said. "Did you see her? Absolutely batshit insane."

"I killed today. I stole. I left a friend behind."

"You saved me. We'll get Ral back." He kissed the back of Teevar's neck and lay back in bed. "Try to sleep," he said softly, but Teevar stayed up and Mac fell asleep on his own.

MAC ROLLED HIS shoulder to try to alleviate the ache as he stood in the kitchen preparing his breakfast. Lenara had taken them around the other side of the planet to keep them on the move but promised again that they'd return for Ral.

She told them she'd take them down on the other side of the city, that she'd land *Veena* farther away and they'd have to keep their faces covered at all times. How they'd find Ral, and how they would get her back once they did find her, Mac didn't know.

He stabbed listlessly at the food on his plate, watching as it turned to mush under his fork. If it had been unappetising before, the thought of putting it in his mouth now made him feel almost overwhelmingly nauseous.

He forced a mouthful down, though it was tasteless and had the consistency of something already chewed, soft and soggy. He looked up when Lenara joined him, managing a small smile that felt like two fishhooks digging into the sides of his mouth.

"How's the arm?" he asked, fork limp in his hand and glad to have a distraction from the food.

"Healed," she said. "Yours?"

"Sore."

"If you need more time to heal before—"

"No. Just get us back down there, Lenara." He abandoned his food and headed back to his room alone. Inside, he pulled off his shirt with a wince and twisted his neck to look at the dark bruising all over the back of his shoulder and side of his arm.

"Ouch." He stripped and went to have a shower.

Later, he sat with Lenara in the cockpit, watching as they descended through the clouds, half-expecting their ship to be blown out of the sky. "We have no plan," he said, after a while.

"Get in unnoticed," Lenara said. "Then we'll go from there."

Mac looked over at her. Her gaze was set and determined. "What if she is dead?"

"She won't be."

"I get the impression that lupa and skreens hate each other. And she took out a lot of them back there. What makes you so certain she's still alive?"

Lenara glanced at him. "Because the lupa and the skreens hate each other," she said. "And they will want her to suffer first."

Lenara brought the ship down in a large expanse of nothingness on the other side of a forest. The three of them disembarked the ship together and walked through the trees. Mac noticed the leaves were perfectly circular and rattled in the wind like castanets. He trudged behind Lenara and Teevar and jogged a little to catch them up.

"We could do with a car," he said. "Or a quad bike. A horse even. I'd settle for a horse. Not that I know how to ride one, but it can't be difficult, right?"

"I don't think we'll find any of those things here," Teevar said, smiling a little. "I'm not even sure what they are."

"No. But a man can dream."

"Shh!" Lenara held up her hand and indicated they should stop walking. Mac couldn't see what had caused her reaction, but his heart began to thump harder anyway. He caught voices ahead and quickly hid behind a tree, peeking out with Teevar by his side—Lenara behind a tree opposite them.

Then he spotted movement, and four jokats each riding a bizarre ostrich-like creature came strolling out of the trees and into the clearing ahead of them. Lenara gestured with her fist, but Mac couldn't work out what the hell she was trying to say. Teevar took his arm and led him away, sneaking through the trees to circle the jokats.

Before Mac could question what was happening, Lenara stepped in front of the party, her weapon held low but threatening.

"We will be needing those ikks," she said, motioning with her gun for them to dismount.

One of the jokats moved forward—the ikk had a weird jerky movement that Mac didn't much like the look of—and twitched his antennae at Lenara. "These are ours," the jokat said. "Step aside."

"We won't be doing that." Mac stepped out behind the jokats, Teevar by his side. "Best do what the lady says and hand them over to us. We wouldn't want anybody to get hurt."

The jokats communicated amongst themselves, mandibles clicking and heads swivelling. Mac had no idea what they were talking about, but they eventually dismounted and backed away with their arms raised.

Lenara shouldered her gun and jumped up onto the back of one the ikk creatures, before leaning over to grab the reins of another. Teevar hopped up onto the back of another and looked to Mac to do the same.

"I don't know how to get up on there," Mac hissed, aware the jokats were still watching.

"Grab the shoulder and jump," Teevar said. "It won't move as soon as you have hold of it."

"Shit." Mac holstered his gun, aware that Teevar pointed his at the jokats, and approached the ikk. Although its body and legs were bird-like, the head of the creature was more reptilian—reminding him of the pictures he'd seen of certain extinct dinosaurs. He wondered if it *was* some sort of dinosaur and then pushed the thought from his head as he lunged for the creature and made a grab at its shoulder.

As Teevar had said, it stopped moving instantly, and Mac managed to haul himself awkwardly onto its back. He clung to the reins, certain he'd fall off if he let go. Before he could ask any questions, like *'how the bloody hell do I make this thing go now?'* Lenara was moving off through the trees, Teevar close behind. Mac's ikk decided it needed to pick up the pace to follow them, and he bounced around on its back feeling distinctly uncool.

"I don't like this!" he yelled. "Teevar!"

Teevar looked back and grinned at him. "Relax. Let your body move with the ikk. Don't try to fight against it."

Mac made an attempt to relax but felt as if he was bouncing around even more, so he clenched his muscles again. "This is not funny. I think we should've walked. This is *not* going to do my arse any favours."

"We'll be there quicker," Lenara said. "And we have a ride to get Ral out. Stop complaining."

"We'll release them as soon as we have Ral," Teevar added. "The jokats will find them again."

"I don't bloody care about the jokats." Mac winced as the movement jolted up through his backside and straight into his shoulder and stared into the forest in moody silence.

It wasn't long before they emerged from the trees and stood before the great expanse of water where the city lay. They covered their faces as best they could and moved forwards, passing through the barrier and into the city once more.

Nobody paid them much attention, luckily, and Mac fancied he was riding a bit steadier now—steady enough that nobody gawked at him anyway. The buildings all looked so similar that he had no idea where they were.

"How are we supposed to find Ral?" he asked.

"They won't have hidden her," Lenara said. "They'll want us to see."

It had been a bright sunny day but, out of nowhere, the rain came down—hard and sudden enough to make Mac gasp. He fussed with his scarf, daring to let go of the reins with one hand, and pulled it up over his head, though it made no difference in keeping him dry.

Water ran down his back and he fidgeted uncomfortably. The weather didn't bother the jokats, and they walked by as if nothing was wrong, but other species dived for cover or hurried by with their heads bowed. Lenara turned them off the main street and dismounted when they came to a quieter area. She waited for Mac and Teevar to do the same, and then they led the ikks on foot.

"Do you know where you're going?" Mac asked.

"No," Lenara said. "Do you?"

"No!"

"I think this place looks familiar," Teevar said.

"Are you sure?" Mac asked. "Because it all looks the same to me." His ikk pulled him aside suddenly and he cried out. He pulled the reins but the creature was too strong for him and dragged him down the street. "Where the hell's this thing going?" he cried.

He kept going, Lenara and Teevar close behind with their ikks pulling them on too, until he came out into a square with a fenced-off area and a load of ikks chirping and pecking at the ground.

"I guess we can park these things here," Mac said.

A kovan, his face red and bad-tempered, came out from under a little stall and approached them. He made an attempt at a smile, but it resembled more of a grimace.

"Fine beasts," he said. "I will be happy to watch over them while you go about your business."

"How much?" Mac asked.

"Four ikks? Eight boule an hour."

"Shove off. Come on, Clover, let's take you elsewhere." Mac was fully aware his ikk had no intention of moving, but he turned away and gave the reins a tug anyway.

"Six," the kovan said. "The best I can do. Help me out, will you? I've got to sit out in this all day."

"You've got a nice little shelter," Mac said, turning back. "You must be raking it in at those prices."

"We don't know how long we'll be," Teevar said, coming forward with money in his hand. "So we'll pay for the day. Thank you."

The kovan gathered up all the reins and took the money with a bow. Mac folded his arms. "Rip off," he muttered.

"It doesn't matter," Teevar said, leading him away. "I just hope he knows which ones are ours when we come to collect them."

"Does *that* matter?" Mac asked. "They all look the same."

The rain eased off as they walked back to the street, but Mac was pretty sure his shoes were already ruined and he was soaked through to his underpants. He rewrapped the scarf so it only covered the lower part of his face and eyed how Lenara had wrapped her silks around her horns—presumably to hide them—though she looked obvious to him.

They stopped when they passed a street closed off and realised it was closed because it led to the bank, and jokats were working to fix the building. Lenara grabbed Mac and Teevar and pulled them back into a recess as a skreen passed by.

Mac held his breath but nobody so much as looked in their direction. "Where are we supposed to find Ral?" he whispered.

"I do not know," Lenara whispered back. "I didn't think they'd take her away."

"What were you expecting? That we were gonna show up and she'd be in stocks or something? Well, she's not here! Don't they have a prison or anything?"

"Hey, guys." Teevar tapped Mac's arm to get his attention and then pointed across the street to where a hologram was beamed onto the front of one of the buildings. It showed Ral, hanging by her arms in a dark room somewhere, her head bowed and one of her ears in tatters. Words scrolled along the bottom of the projection, but Mac couldn't read them.

"What does it say?" he asked. "Does it say where she is? Are they baiting us?"

Teevar moved the scarf from his face, wiped moisture from his skin, and read aloud. "Lupa versus halgranma. Fight to the death. Tomorrow in the arena. Unmissable show. Adults only. Nine boule."

"The arena?" Mac repeated. "So it's gonna be like a gladiator thing? Look at her! She looks half dead! What the bloody hell is a hell grandma?"

"Halgranma," Teevar said. "I...I don't know."

Lenara shook her head when Mac looked at her.

"Great," he said. "At least we have a plan, right? We get ourselves to the arena tomorrow and we bust her the hell out of there. Anybody know where the arena is?"

"We have the rest of the day to find out," Teevar said. He covered his face once more, and the three of them headed out to explore the city.

# Chapter Thirteen

IT TURNED OUT that the arena really wasn't hard to find at all—being right at the heart of the city—and that it was a big deal for the jokats, part of their entertainment or their *only* entertainment after a hard period of work. Mac and the others collected the ikks at the end of the day and rode back to the *Veena*. Nobody stopped them.

"If only we could Google what a halgranma was," Mac said as he followed Lenara and Teevar aboard the ship. "Or maybe it's best we can't do that. It's bound to be something horrific. It'll have five heads, I bet you any money."

Neither Lenara nor Teevar answered him so Mac sighed and decided he'd keep his thoughts to himself. He was only freaking himself out anyway. It was probably best to take his mind off it entirely.

They ate together and then each retired separately to their own rooms. Mac hooked his feet under his bed and performed sit-ups until his stomach hurt. He wondered if he was getting flabby, and he pulled off his shirt to inspect his abs.

A knock at his door made him jump, and he got to his feet to go and see who it was. He opened the door to Teevar and let him inside. "Everything okay?" he asked.

"Didn't want to be on my own," Teevar said. He sighed and sat on the edge of Mac's bed. "Do you think this is my fault?"

"What?" Mac sat beside him. "How is it your fault?"

"I freed her in the first place. She might've been safe if I'd left her where she was. This halgranma thing...what if we can't get to her before it does? What if this whole thing is a set up to get us?"

"It's not your fault. Ral didn't have to come with us after you set her free. She chose to. And we don't know what'll happen tomorrow; we just have to...I don't know. Go with the flow."

"Go with the flow," Teevar repeated. He nodded.

Mac watched as the kovan fiddled with his gold pendant with a glum look on his face. He took hold of his hands to stop him fiddling and kissed him gently on the lips.

"Want me to take your mind off it?" he asked.

Teevar hesitated. "How can we? At a time like this."

Mac kissed him again, taking Teevar's hands and guiding them to his chest and stomach. He pushed him back onto the bed and leaned over him, planting soft kisses along Teevar's jawline and neck. He stopped for long enough to unbutton Teevar's shirt and then continued kissing his chest.

"Mac?"

"Hmm?"

"Mackenzie."

Mac stopped what he was doing and looked at Teevar. "It will be okay," he said. "And if it isn't okay... If it isn't...we'll get through it."

Teevar nodded. They kissed again, and Mac slipped a hand inside Teevar's trousers. He didn't want to think about Ral or discuss it with Teevar or spend the rest of his life worrying about something that might not happen. Teevar's moans were encouraging, so he moved down his body, planting kisses and pulling at Teevar's waistband until his cock was exposed. He sucked him off and then, as Teevar still needed prompting to do things, he took care of his own erection and then lay back, out of breath.

"Wish I was better at this," Teevar said softly, shifting over to lay his head on Mac's chest.

"Plenty of time to learn," Mac said. He kissed the top of Teevar's head and then closed his eyes.


MAC HAD NO idea what time the "unmissable" show was supposed to start, so he and the others left the ship and rode into the city early enough that the sun had only just risen. They split up and scouted around the arena but could see no sign of Ral anywhere. The arena itself—a tall thing made from wood like a giant bathtub—sat right in the centre of the city, surrounded on all sides by the grey stone buildings. A shiver ran down Mac's spine, and he couldn't shake the feeling he was being watched, though every time he looked up at one of the windows, nobody was there.

He met up with Lenara and Teevar again and dismounted from his ikk. "We should leave these things somewhere," he said. "And we should buy some rope or ladders and some explosives or something."

"Tie them up out of the way," Lenara said, pointing to one of the side streets where there was already an ikk tied outside one of the shops. She handed the reins to Mac. "You do that. I will buy explosives. Teevar, get whatever else you think we might need. Meet up back at the gates to the arena."

Mac wasn't impressed with having to deal with the ikks, but Lenara had already walked away. Teevar gave him an apologetic shrug. "I won't be long," he promised, handing over care of his ikk. "Can you manage all four of them?"

"I suppose so. I think they like me now, anyway." Mac gave the reins a tug and led the animals to where the other ikk was. He tied each of them to the railings, feeling a strange fondness for the creatures when one of them nudged him with its nose. "Give over," he said. "I haven't got any food for you." He scratched its neck and then turned and made his way back to the arena.

As he gazed up at the sides of the wooden structure, he wondered if anybody would be checking who entered, waiting for them. If they did manage to make it inside safely, then what? Wait until Ral appeared and leap into the arena, he supposed. Then blast their way the hell out of there. He hoped Lenara bought plenty of explosives.

He was just about to turn away when a cold hand clamped over his mouth and pulled him backwards. Mac screamed, but it was muffled, and he dug his fingernails into the hands holding him, but the skin was thick and it made no difference. He kicked and struggled. Something heavy struck the back of his head, and he saw stars before the ground rushed up to meet him.

When Mac opened his eyes, he couldn't see anything. He scrabbled to his feet with a cry and turned about, eyes wide. He could just make out a slither of light beneath a door, and he grabbed for the handle and pushed and pulled and thumped to no avail. Cursing, he stood back and dragged a hand through his hair. His head pounded.

"Hey!" he yelled. "You can't keep me in here like this!"

Now that his eyes had adjusted, he could see he was in a tiny stone cell, windowless and dusty. A metal bucket sat in one of the corners, and when he inched closer to it, he caught the reek of stale piss.

*Shit. Calm down.* He moved away and took some deep breaths, in through his nose and out through his mouth. His stomach turned over, and he lurched to the side and threw up.

There was a scuff outside the door, a chink of keys, and the door handle turned. Mac backed up, his throat burning and the taste of vomit in his mouth. He quickly shut his eyes as the door opened and light flooded inside.

Squinting, he opened his eyes to see a large male skreen and a smaller, oddly metallic-looking creature, who, judging by its shape, was female.

"Hello," she said, sashaying into the cell. "We've been looking for you."

"You must have the wrong person." Mac eyed the space between the skreen and the door. "I have no idea who you are."

She smiled. She had no hair, no eyebrows, no eyelashes. It didn't look like she had any ears. She almost looked robotic, except she was quite clearly a living, *breathing* being. Mac was all too aware she wore no clothes, although her complete lack of nipples disconcerted him. He made a bolt for the door, but the skreen grabbed him and threw him back into the cell as if he were no more than a rag doll.

He landed heavily on his backside and cried out.

"Now, now, Mackenzie. No more of that." She crouched in front of him and smiled again. "My name's Komeera. I'm a bounty hunter."

"Ah. I don't know who's bothered putting a bounty on me. Probably the skreens, right? Well, I'm here now. They have me. You can just...bugger off."

She touched his cheek and he winced. Her touch was ice cold. "I'm more interested in your friends. They command a higher price. But you and the lupa, you'll do as a little entertainment. The skreens want you to fight. *Halgranma.*"

"Wait, what?" Mac pushed himself to his feet. "I'm not a halgranma. I don't even know what one is. Never heard of it!"

Komeera chuckled. "Halgranma means foreign. Unknown. *You.*"

"Unknown," Mac scoffed. "Obviously I'm kovan."

"Close." Komeera traced a finger down Mac's chest and hooked it into his shirt. She pulled him to her. "But not quite." She pushed him away and stepped back, allowing the skreen to come forward. "Get him ready for the show," she said. "And arm him with something—otherwise he won't last long."

It was only now, as Komeera left, that Mac realised the skreen carried a bucket. He opened his mouth to protest when the skreen sloshed the contents at him. It was warm and sticky and, when he opened his eyes, red. Blood.

His teeth set on edge and he shook droplets of blood from his fingers before wiping a hand across his face. "What the bloody hell?" he exclaimed.

*Lupa versus halgranma*, he thought. *They haven't fed her.*

# Chapter Fourteen

MAC SHIVERED AND clutched the spear he'd been given. The blood had dried now, and his skin felt flaky and disgusting. He picked at his clothes, pulling them away from his body with a grimace. He had to hope Teevar and Lenara had given up looking for him and stuck to the plan of rescuing Ral. Then they could rescue him at the same time.

He looked up as his door opened and menaced his spear at the skreen. "Try it," he warned. "I'll stick you right in the guts."

The skreen grabbed the spear and yanked Mac towards him. Then he grabbed the back of Mac's neck and dragged him from the room. "Save your energy," he warned. "Try to put on a good show. We'll help you make it last as long as possible."

"What the hell does that mean?" Mac asked, struggling to keep up as the skreen pulled him along. He passed Komeera, and she gave him an insultingly wide smile.

"You're a psycho," he hissed at her. "I won't fight Ral! She won't fight me!"

"You'll be surprised," Komeera said.

The skreen stopped outside metal gates, and with a bark at two of his companions, waited as they pulled a chain to bring the barrier up. Mac's heart thumped loud in his ears, but even over that he could hear shouts and cheers coming from the audience in the arena.

Once the gate was lifted, the skreen shoved him forward. Mac stumbled, righted himself, and turned in time to see the gate come crashing down, sealing him inside. He turned to the arena. The wooden walls towered over him; the jokats looking much more ant-like from their seats. Opposite him there was another metal gate, and halfway around the arena to his right, yet another one.

"God," he muttered. He gripped his spear and moved out farther into the arena, scanning the crowd in the hope of seeing Teevar or Lenara. A cold shiver ran over him as he wondered if they'd been caught too.

The jokats—and yes, there were other species in the crowd too, he noticed—jeered and thumped their fists, looking just like a bunch of bizarre alien football supporters. Slowly, they began stamping their feet, out of rhythm at first, until they all got in time and banged out a very sinister *thump, thump, thump.*

*"Halgranma!"* The announcement sounded as if it came over a loudspeaker, though Mac couldn't see one. Holographic images flashed up all over the walls of the arena, showing himself blood-covered and wide-eyed, turning around to take it all in. "Versus lupa!"

Images flashed again, showing Ral this time. She stood on all fours with her ears pinned back and fur standing on end. She looked half-mad. Mac pulled his attention from the holograms when he realised it was showing *live* and that she was there in the arena with him, *opposite* him, and she looked more than happy to kill him.

"Ral!" he called. "It's me! It's Mac!"

Ral stood up. Her teeth were bared and her eyes flashed dangerously. Mac held his spear tight and braced himself as she ran at him.

*Wait,* he told himself. *Wait, wait, wait.*

Ral leapt just before she reached him, and Mac dived and rolled out of the way. She turned and he pointed the spear at her again, warning her to keep back. "I don't want to hurt you," he said. "I'm here to rescue you." He noticed a collar at her neck, a small light flashing, and it made him frown.

Ral didn't speak. She snarled at him and leapt again. Mac turned his spear, caught Ral in the shoulder with the blunt end, and shoved her past with a yell.

"Wake up!" he yelled at her.

She ran around him and he spun to keep her at his front, but then she came in quick and sudden and was inside the range of his spear before he could react. He cried out and she bowled into him, knocking him to the ground. He used his spear haft awkwardly to keep her back, to keep her teeth away from his face as she snapped at him.

"Shitting hell!" he yelled. "Teevar!"

He twisted the haft, bringing the end up to knock the side of Ral's head. She grunted and he took advantage of her momentary lapse by smacking her again and turning her round so he was now on top. He straddled her, using his full weight to hold her down while she struggled and snapped her jaws at him. Images changed on the walls, and he noticed it showed more creatures rushing into the arena—these ones like bulked-up versions of the jokats. He spotted three of them running towards him and Ral, and he yelled at her to stop struggling. Quickly, he sawed at the collar around her neck with the spear until it snapped and fell away.

Ral's eyes cleared and she stopped struggling. "Mac?" she said.

"Hi. You okay?"

"You smell so good," she said. "I'm *so* hungry."

"Yeah, hold that thought for a bit." He jumped off her and held out a hand to help haul her to her feet.

The two of them turned to face the new threat, but the jokats were on them suddenly. Mac cried out and only half-managed to divert a blow with his spear.

"I knew they'd send more in, the bastards!" Mac yelled, striking out with his spear again. "Where the bloody hell are Teevar and Lenara?"

"*Mac*! Mac!"

Mac struck out at another assailant, stabbing the creature between the shoulder and thorax. He looked up at the sound of his name and saw Teevar running down through the audience to lean over the wall.

"Hold on!" Teevar yelled. "We couldn't get explosives!"

"Bounty hunters are here," Mac yelled back. He punched a jokat in the face when it came too close for him to use his spear.

"Get to the gate!" Teevar yelled.

"Get to the bloody gate," Mac muttered, wrestling a jokat off him and menacing it with the spear once it was down. He looked for Ral and saw her tear off a jokat's arm with her teeth. More of the creatures were racing towards them now, and Mac whistled to get Ral's attention.

"To the gate, Ral, leave them!"

Mac didn't need to ask which gate. Lights flashed where Lenara stood outside the arena, blasting the metal with her gun. He looked up to the audience again and saw Teevar also running in the same direction, but there were skreens swarming through the crowds to get to him now.

He wanted to cry out to him, to warn him, but figured he was well aware and he needed to save his breath. His lungs burned and his muscles screamed at him, but he reached the gate in time to see Lenara lower her weapon.

"Get us out of here, Lenara."

"Move back," she said. "I think I've weakened it enough."

He stepped back as she lowered her head and rammed her horns into the metal. He turned to see Ral scuffling with two of the giant jokats and, incensed, he ran towards them and launched his spear as if it were a javelin. It wobbled through the air and struck one of the creatures in the side. Ral broke free and ran towards him, and he turned back as the gate buckled and bent with a crash.

"Hurry," Lenara said, pulling him through.

"What about Teevar?" Mac cried, running out behind the arena to look up at the walls. "Teevar! Teevar!"

Ral had squeezed through the gap, and Lenara was firing her weapon again. Mac stared up at the heights of the wall, heart in his mouth.

A rope was thrown over the edge, and then Teevar appeared, climbing over the side.

"Mac, the ikks," Lenara called. "Get the ikks!"

Mac didn't want to move away in case Teevar needed him. He cursed loudly and then yelled at Ral, "Down there. They're down there. Go and get them; don't eat them!"

Teevar was almost halfway down when a skreen head appeared over the wall. He looked up at it and then back down at Mac.

"Keep going, just keep going!" Mac called. "Come on."

Other skreens appeared at the top of the wall, and one pushed the first aside and went to the rope, a knife in his hand. He sawed at the rope, causing it to fray and snap.

Teevar cried out. Mac gasped. Lenara was still shooting.

*Keep going.* Mac willed Teevar to move, but he seemed frozen. *I can't catch him.*

Ikks surrounded Mac, bobbing their heads and making odd jerky movements in their panic. Ral bounded past, leapt at the wall and for Teevar just as the rope snapped, and he yelled out. She caught him and they fell together. There was a horrible world-stopping moment when they hit the ground together in a roll, and they were still. Then Teevar was up and helping Ral to her feet.

Mac broke out of his daze. He snatched at the reins of the nearest ikk, then made a grab for the others. "Come on," he yelled. "Lenara, time to go!"

Teevar and Ral mounted up next to him, the ikks skittish and ready to go. Lenara shouldered her gun and turned from the gate; she ran for her ikk and jumped onto its back. "They're coming," she said. "Ride fast."

Mac held on tight and urged his ikk into a run. He chanced a look back over his shoulder and saw the buckled gate had jammed and skreens and beefed-up jokats were squeezing underneath. He didn't look back again.

The four of them rode together, dodging and weaving through the city, keeping a good lead on their pursuers. They didn't stop running, didn't allow the ikks to let up, even once they were free of the city and racing through the forest. None of them spoke.

Mac could see the ship now, and his heart leapt. There was nobody around it, nobody following them. He pulled on the reins and brought his ride to a skidding halt, his heart pulsing in his ears. He laughed then, when the others joined him, and Teevar gave him a reluctant grin in return.

"Don't celebrate just yet," Lenara said, dismounting. She clapped to shoo the ikk away and opened up the *Veena*. "Let's get us in the air first."

"Right." Mac dismounted and pushed his ikk away, a twinge of guilt stirring in his gut when the animal turned back to him. "Go on home," he said. "Go on."

Ral practically fell from her mount and Teevar hurried to her side to hold her up. Mac joined him and together they helped the lupa aboard.

"Need to eat," she muttered, as they practically dragged her inside.

"I think you need to rest," Mac said. Ral snapped at him and he jumped back. "Okay, food first."

Lenara left them to it, running off to the cockpit. Mac and Teevar helped Ral into the kitchen and plonked her onto one of the chairs, before grabbing any meat they could from the stores. Mac watched, nose screwed up in distaste as Ral crunched through bone and raw meat.

"We should leave her to it," Teevar said, his voice soft. "Once she's done, she can sleep and then I'll sort out her wounds when she's ready. This will help to replenish her strength."

They left the kitchen and walked out into the corridor. "Are you all right?" Mac asked.

Teevar nodded. "Just shaken. You?"

"Bruised, battered. Filthy. I need to have a shower before I do anything else."

They kissed briefly before parting ways. Mac stripped off, dumped his clothes, and went straight into his shower, shuddering at the blood running off him. He scrubbed his hair and his skin and stood under the warm water until he was almost falling asleep. He dried himself and returned to his bed, where he slept as soon as his head hit the pillow.

# Chapter Fifteen

MAC WOKE SOMETIME later. The ship was quiet as he wandered through the corridors and made his way to the cockpit. Lenara wasn't there and the ship floated idle. He hoped they were far enough away from the planet that nobody was coming after them. He sat in the pilot seat and eyed the controls but didn't touch them.

He must've fallen asleep again because he jumped out of his skin when somebody touched him on the shoulder. Ral sat next to him and she flashed him her teeth.

"You look better," he said, rubbing his face.

"I feel better," she said. "But I still hurt." She touched her torn and scarred ear. "Does this look okay?"

"Yeah," Mac said. "Suits you."

Ral smiled. They sat quietly for a little while, staring out of the window. Eventually Ral said, "You were very brave back there."

"Couldn't let you kill me," Mac joked. He sighed. "Ral, I met one of the bounty hunters. Komeera. She didn't seem that interested in me or you—she was happy for the skreens to kill us—but she wants Lenara and Teevar."

"She won't get them."

"I know; we keep running." He glanced sidelong at her and then back out the window. "We'd be safe on Earth. I'd look after you."

"I believe you would try."

Mac leaned back against the seat and didn't argue. He'd talk to Teevar and convince him to convince the others it was the best thing to do. He didn't know how much more he could fight if the bounty hunters, or the skreens, caught up with him again.

"How much did we get from the bank?" Ral asked.

Mac perked up. "I don't think anybody's counted," he said. "With everything going on, I'd sort of...forgotten."

"Shall we count now?"

"Too right."

Mac and Ral left the cockpit together and headed down into the cargo bay. Mac was surprised to see Teevar already down there, stacking up coins and blocks of boule. The kovan looked up as they came down the stairs.

"You should both be resting," Teevar said.

"Rested enough," Mac replied. He joined Teevar and peered into one of the bags. "We got quite a haul, eh?"

"I'm afraid I don't know the value of some of these items." Teevar opened up a bag and showed Mac an array of jewellery. "I hope none of this had sentimental value."

"If it meant that much to someone, they wouldn't have stuck it in a bank out of sight." Mac reached into the bag and pulled out a chain of blue jewels that sparkled and flashed in the light. "This has got to be worth a pretty penny."

"Do we have enough to pay off the hunters?" Ral asked.

Teevar shrugged. "Maybe. I don't know." He looked at Mac suddenly, worry written all over his handsome face. "Did they do anything to you when they had you captive? Anything at all?"

Mac frowned. "I don't think so," he said. "They threw blood over me and forced me to fight Ral. That's bad enough, isn't it?"

"Yes, yes." Teevar patted Mac down and then felt around his head and behind his ears; he ran his hands through Mac's hair.

"Much as I'm enjoying this, we could probably take it somewhere more private," Mac commented. "What are you looking for?"

Teevar peered into Mac's eyes, studying them. "I want to know if they've tagged you."

Mac pulled back, alarmed. "In my eyeballs?"

"I don't know. Anywhere."

"Shit." Mac glanced back at Ral. "They could've tagged the pair of us, right? I mean, what do you mean exactly...*tagged*? They could be tracking us?" He wondered if the kovans had put a tracker in his thigh.

Teevar nodded. He took the jewels from Mac and put them back in the bag. "Let me check both of you over in the medical bay. I can run a scan to see if there's anything...internal."

*Internal?* Mac felt sick to his stomach and violated all over again. He followed Teevar and Ral to the medical bay, waving Teevar away when he turned to him. "Ral first."

He folded his arms as Ral sat herself on the edge of the bed. Teevar took a handheld scanner and ran it over the lupa's body. Then he checked again, just in case.

"Nothing," he said.

"They were probably expecting us to kill each other, right?" Mac took his turn on the bed. "What's the point in tagging us if we'd just end up as corpses?"

"You're probably right." Teevar frowned in concentration over the scanner. He indicated for Mac to stand and moved around him again, stopping behind his back.

"What?" Mac asked, trying to gauge Ral's reaction as he couldn't see Teevar's. "What? You've gone quiet. Have you found something?"

"Maybe."

"What do you mean *maybe*?"

"The scan indicates there is a foreign body in your neck. You don't have any...modifications?"

"No. Modifications? Gross. No, of course not. Wait, it's not the translator chip, is it?"

"I'm not sure. It could be. Usually it'd be a little higher up, but I suppose it could've migrated."

Mac groaned and sat on the bed again. "I am *not* okay with people putting things inside my body. Definitely not without my permission. Can you...get it out?"

Teevar smiled and squeezed Mac's hand. "Of course. You're in safe hands."

"I will go and wake Lenara," Ral said. "If it's a tracking device, we need to move."

Teevar nodded distractedly. He put the scanner down and picked up a scalpel instead. "There is a numbing agent in the blade," he said. "This won't hurt."

"Great." Mac gripped the edge of the bed anyway and braced himself for any pain. The tip of the knife touched his skin and then he felt nothing. He waited. Teevar wiped something across his neck—cleaning the blood away.

"There's something there?" Mac asked.

No reply.

"Teevar? Is there something there or not?"

"Yes. But."

"But?"

"I don't know if I can remove it. It looks like it's attached."

"Attached to *what*?"

"Attached to the bone."

Mac blanched. He swallowed hard and reached up to the back of his neck to feel what Teevar could see. "Is it transmitting anything? How can we get rid of it? We can't cut my head off!"

"I can knock you out. I'll be able to see properly if I can remove it—I will be able to remove it."

Mac pulled away to look at Teevar. "You're not a surgeon. And you know nothing about human biology—one slip in that area and you could paralyse me."

Teevar looked down at the blood covered scalpel in his hand. "You're right. Let me close up the wound and we'll think of another way. Maybe we can muffle the signal somehow."

Mac sat back again, frowning to himself as Teevar began work on his neck. Whatever numbing agent coated the blade meant he couldn't feel the laser knitting his skin back together, which he was thankful for. A wave of light-headedness washed over him and he closed his eyes.

MAC'S HEAD POUNDED. He squinted into the light and blinked until he could see properly. He was still in the medical bay, and the back of his neck ached dully. He made to sit up.

"No, no." Teevar pushed him gently back down. "Just rest now, Mac."

Mac wanted to speak but didn't quite have the energy to form words. He noticed a pile of bloodied rags on the side behind Teevar and something metallic and glistening.

He sucked in a breath. "You did it," he said. "You *operated* on me. Without my permission." He sat up, ignoring the head spin and glared at the kovan. "How *dare* you."

"Please lie down. You'll hurt yourself."

Mac smacked Teevar's hand away. "I can't believe you," he snapped. "Who the hell do you think you are? You had no idea what you were doing; you could've paralysed me, hell, Teevar, you could've *killed* me."

"I'm sorry. I had to get that thing out of you, and I had to knock you out—"

"You didn't have to do anything!" Mac glared at Teevar, his hands shaking with fury, unable to quite believe that he would do that to him. The betrayal struck him like a knife. "I trusted you."

Teevar looked down at his hands. "I truly am sorry. I had no other choice. The bounty hunters could've found us—"

"They could still find us," Mac hissed, getting up off the bed. He went to the transmitting device and turned it over, pleased there wasn't any bone stuck to it at least. He smacked his fist down on it until it smashed. "They'll know where we are, and they're probably coming after us right now. We had *time* to find somewhere safe and have the operation performed by a real doctor."

"We had *no* time." Teevar held out his hands, imploring Mac to...to what? To calm down? To see his point of view?

Mac shook his head. "Don't speak to me again, Teevar. I never would've done anything like this to you." He stomped towards the door, but Teevar caught his arm and turned him back. The kovan's face was red with anger.

"I had *no choice*. And come on, Mac, you're no innocent. You've hurt me."

"When?"

"You and Eesha."

Mac laughed. "I had a fumble with someone else, so what? You could've killed me!"

He stormed out before he did something he regretted. Teevar called after him, "You're overreacting!" but he ignored him and carried on.

Mac slammed the door to his room and then opened it and slammed it again for good measure. He rested his forehead against the door and sobbed, the tears coming before he could stop them. He bellowed a curse, kicked the door, and then sat on his bed.

"Shit," he muttered, softly. He brushed the back of his neck with his fingertips but could feel no scar.

Wiping his eyes, he lay back. *How could he do that to me? Bastard. You let yourself care too much, Mac.*

*Earth.* He had to get back to Earth, on his own. Let the others do whatever the hell they wanted now, he'd done his bit. They could take him back and that would be the end of it. He sniffed and folded his arms across his chest, staring up at the ceiling.

*I'm done.*

HE MUST'VE FALLEN asleep, but he woke at a tap on his door. He didn't answer, didn't call out. Somebody scuffed behind the door and put something on the floor before their footsteps disappeared away down the corridor. Mac knew it had been Teevar. He waited a moment longer before getting up and opening the door. There was a tray of food there and a note that read *Sorry*.

Mac scowled at the tray. And then he realised the note was written in English. He picked up the tray and took it into his room, sitting down with it on his bed.

*He learnt English.* He stared at the note, not quite sure what he felt about that. They'd spent plenty of time together just chatting into the night, showing each other drawings of their home worlds and making scribblings in the notepad. That Teevar had actually remembered things, had paid enough attention to learn a little of a completely alien language... He snatched the note and balled it up. Teevar had operated on him without his permission—that was a whole new level of relationship-crazy he couldn't deal with. He ate the food though and then chucked the tray back out into the corridor, making sure the wrinkled note was visible on top. He went back to bed and slept undisturbed for a good few hours.

When he woke again, his head felt much better. He strode out of his room and straight to the cockpit, where he met with Lenara. She turned briefly to see who had entered.

"Is anybody following us?" he asked.

"Not immediately."

"I want you to take me back to where you first found me. I've had enough, Lenara. I've done enough. It's time for me to go home."

"I can take you back to Cernod," she said. "But it is dangerous, Mackenzie. Back on that planet, you were running scared. You are so convinced this pin of yours can take you back to Earth, but you don't know where it is, or if it even still exists."

"I'll find it. You can't be against this. You were all for coming to Earth with me before."

Lenara sighed. "I will help you. I promise you that."

Mac nodded. "Thanks. I'll get out of your hair." He turned and left the cockpit before he thought too much on what Lenara had said. He pushed it all from his mind and instead made his way to the star room so he could gaze out at the universe and forget about everything.

He let out an audible groan upon entering the room and finding Teevar already there, and he turned to leave.

"Mac?"

"Don't worry, I'll leave you to it."

"No, don't go. Can we talk?"

Mac turned back. "About what? You hurt me, Teevar. You betrayed me."

"I know. I know!" Teevar approached him and reached for him, but Mac raised his hands, stopping him from coming any closer. "I'm sorry. I'm so sorry. I hate that you're pushing me away like this. I didn't want to hurt you, and please believe me when I say I'd never have put you under if I truly thought I could've damaged you. I was so certain I could remove the device and I did!"

"Then *talk* to me. Convince me; don't just do it anyway!"

"I know that now." Teevar clutched at his pendant, a desperate look on his face. "I was so frightened they'd find us."

Mac laughed. "Yeah, worried about yourself. Of course."

"Yes, worried for myself! But terrified for you. I couldn't bear the thought of them taking you again. When Lenara and I lost you at the arena, when we saw the signs of a struggle, I…"

"You?"

Teevar closed his eyes. "I broke down. I threatened to kill myself."

Mac folded his arms. "Well, that's a bit dramatic. You could've tried saving me before topping yourself."

"That's almost exactly what Lenara said." Teevar offered him a small, embarrassed smile.

Mac shrugged. *Teevar cares.* He cared more about him than anybody ever had before. Surely that meant something? "You do anything like that to me ever again," he warned.

"I won't." Teevar reached for Mac's hand, and Mac let him take it before gently freeing himself.

"Give me time to calm down. Okay? Just give me some time."

Teevar nodded. He passed Mac and slipped quietly out of the room. Mac sat amongst Teevar's incense and closed his eyes briefly. There was an ache in his chest that he didn't want to have to deal with. *You wouldn't even consider forgiving him if you didn't love him*, he told himself. *I love him.*

"But I need to go home."

# Chapter Sixteen

THEY HAD THREE days of peace aboard the *Veena*. Ral recovered, Mac's mood lifted, and he and Teevar spent more time together—although they did little more than talk, and Lenara told them she'd found a space station where they could sell some of their items and make a little more boule.

Mac sat in the cockpit once more, gaping at the space station as Lenara manoeuvred the *Veena* for docking. The station towered before them, delving down into the depths of space and rising high above. Other ships flew all around, landing and leaving. The station's engines jutted out at intervals along the column, like shiny metal testicles, and Mac only found out they were engines when he asked Lenara what the hell those globular things were.

"There's got to be lots going on in there, right?" he asked. "I mean, we can stay for a bit, right?"

Lenara smiled. "We can stay for a while," she confirmed. "We'll find the best price for our goods. We can eat and sleep and entertain ourselves aboard the station. There will be lots for us to do."

"Brilliant."

The ship jolted as it locked into place in one of the station's ports and then Lenara turned off the engines. They all left the ship together and emerged into a large open area, very much like the inside of an airport. Only *bigger*. And shinier. Aliens bustled about around them, and robots zoomed past carrying baggage. A calming female voice welcomed them over a loudspeaker.

Mac grinned. "This is my favourite place so far. Please tell me I can spend some money?"

"We should probably make some money first," Teevar replied.

"Pfft. Later. Hey, Ral? Come and look at this!" He peeled off with Ral, and left Lenara and Teevar to their own devices. He'd spotted what looked like a giant glass tube running across the room, filled with water and creatures swimming through.

"Those are the banyu," Ral said, smiling in bemusement. "Probably best not to stare at them."

Mac stared anyway. The banyu were like elongated jellyfish with green, insect-like eyes, and strangely pulsating bodies. "They're people? Can they talk?"

"I suppose so," Ral said. "I've never spoken to one. They never leave the water."

"What are they doing in space?"

"No idea."

Mac laughed. "Wish I had a camera. You have no idea what this is all like for me. Seeing all this stuff, this *amazing* stuff, it's what dreams are made of. Try to imagine seeing something you've never seen before."

"I'd like to see Earth," Ral said. "If you'll take me."

Mac looked at her in surprise. "Absolutely! I always said I would." He gave her a nudge. "Come on, let's get back to the others and flog this stuff."

It turned out that Lenara had discovered a group of veneks aboard the space station and was more than happy to do business with them without the help of the others—in fact she practically insisted they bugger off and leave her to it—so Mac, Teevar, and Ral handed over anything they had on them to sell and set off to explore the station.

They walked down clean, white corridors, with curved walls and ceilings, and sellers nestled in nooks in the walls. Ral bought some grim-looking roasted insects and proceeded to pick the legs off them and crunch them in front of Mac, who pulled a face and turned away.

They walked on. Teevar put his hand to the small of Mac's back and pointed out another stallholder selling shiny trinkets and, even though Mac hadn't let Teevar get too close since the operation, he didn't push him away. That small gesture of affection in public made him strangely touched.

"Let me buy you something," Teevar said.

"I don't need you to buy me anything."

"I want to."

They approached the stall and looked at the goods spread out on the table—tiny sparkling jewels carved into the shapes of people, rings and pendants, delicate blades with intricate handles. Teevar picked up a gold oval pendant and showed it to Mac. "This one," he said.

"That's not a religious thing, is it?"

Teevar's cheeks grew red. "It's a kovan symbol of love. Where I'm from we give them as gifts to family members or…" He cleared his throat. "…or lovers."

"All right." Mac folded his arms as Teevar paid for the pendant, trying not to look too bothered about it all, though he did smile when Teevar fastened it around his neck. The smallest spasm of guilt touched his stomach, that he'd been so distant of late.

Ral munched her disgusting insect-popsicle, watching them both. "I'm going to see if there are any lupa aboard," she said. "Preferably male." She tapped her comms device, which she'd fastened to a belt around her hips. "Call me if you need me."

"We will," Mac said. "Have fun."

Once she'd left, he wrapped his fist around his pendant and then popped it inside his shirt. "How do you think Lenara's getting on?" he asked.

"I can call her and find out?"

Mac shook his head. "Nah, don't interrupt her. She might be in the middle of a deal." He took hold of Teevar's hand—mostly to test his reaction—and wandered down the corridor with him.

Although Teevar didn't protest, Mac could tell he was uncomfortable. Eventually, Teevar pulled his hand away in the pretence of picking up a roll of fabric from one of the stalls.

"Nobody cares, you know," Mac said.

Teevar smiled. "What do you mean?"

"That we were holding hands. Nobody was looking. Nobody gives a shit."

"I'm sorry."

"Stop apologising."

"So—" Teevar stopped himself and gave Mac an apologetic grin. He put the fabric down, looking around to see if anybody was looking at them, and then took Mac's hand again. "What do you want to do now?"

Mac let his gaze travel down Teevar's body. "I can think of a few things."

"Really? Oh, you mean…" He cleared his throat. "I'll find us a room."

Mac smirked. He'd let Teevar embarrass himself asking for a room for the pair of them—he deserved that at least. Info booths were dotted throughout the station and Teevar waited at one while a smiley attendant handed him a map and a key card. Mac threw an arm around Teevar's shoulders, just to make it clear what they wanted the room for.

"Um...so." Teevar walked stiffly away from the booth and opened the map. A hologram popped up, showing the entire inside of the space station. Teevar touched one of the sections and the image changed, showing a closer view. "This is where we are now. We go left just ahead."

Teevar folded the map away, and they headed off to find the rooms. Mac raised his eyebrows when they got there. The rooms were no more than pods built into the walls, reminding him of pictures he'd seen of a futuristic Japanese hotel. Teevar fumbled with his key card and swiped it at the door of the nearest empty pod. The door opened with an impressive *swoosh*.

"Cosy," Mac commented, peering inside.

The floor of the pod was the bed. There was a holo-screen at the back of the pod, a couple of shelves to either side, and not much else at all. Mac clambered inside and waited for Teevar to join him. "You're not claustrophobic, are you?" he asked as the door closed.

"I'm not sure what that is," Teevar admitted, fidgeting to get comfortable.

"Fear of confined spaces."

"Oh. Then no."

Mac manoeuvred himself on top of Teevar, pulse racing, and placed soft kisses across his jawline.

"Mac?"

"Mm?"

"Does this mean you've forgiven me?"

"This means I'm horny." He sighed and pulled back to look at Teevar. The wide-eyed expression on the other man's face made his heart swell. "You're forgiven, okay? I don't see the point in staying angry forever. I don't have the energy."

"Okay." Teevar reached up to touch Mac's face. "Good."

Mac smiled, and they kissed again.

# Chapter Seventeen

MAC TURNED TO help Teevar from the pod and then fussed with his hair and clothes until he felt less of a scruff. He touched his comms. "Lenara? How are you getting on?"

Teevar swiped the card and the pod closed up once more. He raised his eyebrows at Mac when there was no answer and tried his own device. "Lenara?"

"She's ignoring us, right?" Mac said. "She's probably right in the middle of the deal. Or she's found a fit venek bloke to cop off with."

"I don't think Lenara would do that."

Mac touched his comms again. "Lenara? Let us know if you're okay." He gazed at Teevar, noting the worried frown on the other man's face. "Lenara?"

"We should go back to where we left her. See if we can find her."

They hurried back to the large welcome bay just off where they'd docked and scanned the crowd for Lenara. Teevar spotted the veneks she'd traded with, but Lenara wasn't with them. He headed over before Mac could stop him.

"Have you seen our friend?" Teevar asked as he approached. There were three of them, two females and a male. The biggest of them stepped forward.

"Your friend, little kovan? We do not know your friend. Try sector six. I hear there are many more kovans there."

"She's a venek," Mac said. "Lenara. She was with you earlier."

"Ah." The venek clicked her teeth. "She left us after we made our deal, though we invited her to eat with us this evening."

"Do you know where she went?" Mac asked, beginning to get annoyed. "She's not answering her comms."

The venek visibly bristled; she thrust out her chest and lifted her chin. "Maybe she wishes for some peace and quiet from little ones."

"Hey, I'm not much shorter than you," Mac said, jabbing a finger at her. "Just tell us which direction she went in at least, eh?"

The venek pointed. Mac looked at the direction she indicated and then headed off, leaving Teevar to say thank you and follow. Mac touched his comms. "Ral, we've lost Lenara. Put down whatever you're playing with and come and find us."

"She could be anywhere," Teevar said, hurrying to keep up with him. "What if something's happened to her? If she's had an accident?"

"Well aren't there medics here? Maybe we should start there—at a hospital or something."

"Good idea." Teevar pulled out his map and flicked through various images, frowning over them and not looking where he was going. Mac grabbed his arm and pulled him out the way as a robot trolley dolly wheeled by.

The movement caused him to look to his left, and he did a double take when he spotted skreens across the way, disappearing down one of the corridors. Between them, unmistakably, walked Lenara. Mac tugged Teevar's hand and hurried after them, keeping back a good distance.

"What? What's happening?" Teevar asked.

"Lenara. With skreens."

"A prisoner? Did she look okay?"

"I don't know. I think so. I only caught a glimpse." He touched his comms again. "Ral, where the bloody hell are you?"

Ral's voice came back to him. "Stay where you are. I'll find you."

"We can't stay where we are. We're following Lenara. She's with the skreens." He'd lost sight of them now, but they couldn't have gone anywhere else so he carried on down the corridor until it ended and split in two different directions. He stopped abruptly and dragged a hand through his hair.

"Which way?" Teevar asked.

"I don't know. Shit!" He spotted Ral, then, appearing at the end of the corridor, and he raised his arm to get her attention.

"Where's Lenara?" Ral asked when she joined them. "I can smell she's been this way."

"Can you track her?" Mac asked. "Which way now? We'll follow you."

Ral sniffed the air and chose the right-hand corridor. She strode ahead, and Mac and Teevar marched determinedly behind her.

"They'll be docked somewhere," Teevar said. "They could be taking her straight to their ship. What do the skreens want with Lenara?"

"They're working with Komeera," Mac said. "The bounty hunter. I bet that bitch is here somewhere. I bet she tracked me!"

"But I removed the device."

"I bloody know you did! But she must've followed us so far and then... I don't bloody know. Maybe there's another one in me. Maybe there's one in Ral and you missed it. What the hell do we do now?"

"We should leave," Ral said. "Blow the whole place up. Then they'll never come after us again."

"Are you out of your fucking mind?" Mac snapped. "There's god knows how many people in here, and we're not blowing up Lenara. Besides, we don't *have* any bloody explosives."

"We should bargain with them," Teevar said. "Give them the money."

"Right. That was the plan all along, right? Do you think it'll work?"

Teevar sighed. "I don't know. I hope so."

The corridor opened out into a dining area, packed with people. Some of the tables were out in the open, others hidden in private booths. Mac scanned the faces but couldn't see Lenara.

"Is she here?" he asked Ral.

"Too many other smells," Ral said. "I can't tell."

"We'll never find them. We need them to find us." Mac approached the nearest table, apologised to the diners, and clambered up onto it, knocking their plates with his feet. "Hey, Komeera?" he yelled. "You here? We're all here. Why don't you come and get us? Komeera?"

"Mac." Teevar tugged Mac's trouser leg and pointed out two orange-skinned aliens, weaving between the tables to reach them. Mac didn't know if they were staff or law enforcement.

He pulled his gun on them. "Stop right there, gents. We're not here to cause trouble, we just want to speak to Komeera. You seen her? Crazy silver bitch who likes to stick tracking devices in people's necks."

The men stopped advancing and gave each other an uncertain look before one started backing up, with his hands raised. Mac was fairly certain he'd be arrested soon. "Stop," he warned him. "Nobody move; nobody do anything. Komeera, you in here?"

Diners murmured amongst themselves. Some carried on eating, clearly not bothered by Mac's display. He searched their faces, not quite sure what to do next.

Then, "Put the gun away, Mackenzie." Komeera emerged from one of the booths, a smile on her face as she sauntered towards him. She raised a hand. "There's no need for tantrums."

"Where's Lenara?" Teevar demanded. "What have you done with her?"

Komeera's gaze slid from Mac to the kovan and her smile widened. "Would you like to see her? You're welcome aboard my ship. In fact, I suggest you all come with me, quickly, before you end up in any more trouble."

Mac pointed his gun at her head. *I could shoot her and end this now*, he thought.

"Don't be silly," Komeera said. "Killing me will not get you your friend back and it will not stop others coming after you."

"We'll bargain with you," Mac said. "We have money."

"After the stunt you pulled on Iona-Ra, I'm sure you do. Please put the gun away and join me aboard my ship. You have my word I'll not take you anywhere until I've listened to your offer."

Mac hesitated. He looked at Teevar, who nodded. He thrust his gun back into its holster and jumped off the table. "Fine. Lead the way."

Komeera inclined her head and turned away, leaving them to follow after her. Mac noticed the wary looks he got as he passed by the other diners and staff.

Soon, they entered into another corridor again and headed towards a pair of closed doors Mac presumed was a lift. He looked at Ral, wondering if this really was the way they took Lenara and she, understanding what he was thinking, nodded.

The lift doors slid open and the four of them entered together. Mac's heart thumped as he wondered if they were being led into a trap.

"I'm a business woman," Komeera said. "Interested only in money. I'll not harm any of you."

"You made me and Ral fight each other," Mac said. "Sorry, but I'm not going to trust you anytime soon."

"That was what the skreens wanted. You can hardly blame them."

"Yes I can!"

Teevar took hold of Mac's hand and gave it a squeeze to calm him down. Mac bit his tongue and said no more in case he endangered any of them by saying something stupid. They didn't have to follow Komeera for long before she led them to where her ship was docked—a ship that was easily five times the size of the *Veena*. Mac couldn't tell if it was the same ship that had tried to reel them in previously, but it looked remarkably similar.

They boarded and didn't stop to look at anything as Komeera led them straight in and up into the heart of the ship. Mac had been expecting futuristic curves and LED lights, but he was faced with stark metal and harsh lines. A couple of skreens passed them, but there were also other species—none of whom looked like Komeera.

"This your crew?" Mac asked.

"We are a bit of a mix," Komeera said. "I don't discriminate." She paused to tap numbers into a keypad and open a door.

Lenara sat inside and she looked up as they entered. Mac didn't fail to notice she was cuffed. "What are you doing here?" she asked.

"Came to rescue you," Mac said. "Obviously."

"We're here to bargain for your release," Teevar clarified.

Lenara clicked her teeth. "Do you not think I've offered them money? Now she has all of us!"

They spun around. Komeera raised her hands, a smile on her face. "I will take your money," she said. "I have already sent men to retrieve it from your ship. It's more than I would get from Nevka for Lenara's return, and it is more than the skreens were offering for Mac and Ral. But, Teevar Nok Dimar, your people *really* want you home to face justice. You are a priest and you are a murderer. Did you really think they'd let you go so easily?"

"We're not leaving without Teevar!" Mac exclaimed, pointing his gun at Komeera. By his side, Ral bared her teeth.

"Weapons do not work aboard my ship," Komeera said. "Please do try it."

Mac did try it. His gun clicked but didn't fire. He cursed. "Bite her, Ral! Bloody bite her!"

As Ral rushed forwards, Komeera raised a hand and the lupa dropped like a stone. "Of course I have safeguards in place," Komeera said. "She is quite all right."

Teevar knelt by Ral's side and helped her up as she came around. Mac gaped. "What did you do to her? What else did you do to me when you had me prisoner? Can you control me like that if I come at you? You're an absolute bloody psycho!"

"Your physiology is so simple, I'd be afraid to damage you if I tried anything like that with you. Now, please stop trying to attack me. You are—"

She stopped when a member of her crew appeared and tapped her on the shoulder. They turned away and spoke quietly together.

Mac frowned as he caught Komeera say the words, "Much blood? I'll be right there."

He opened his mouth as Komeera turned back, but she gestured with her hand and the door closed in his face. He didn't fail to notice her worried expression first though.

"You three are idiots," Lenara said.

"You're the one who got caught," Ral replied.

Teevar joined the girls, leaving Mac staring at the door. "You three should go," he said. "Leave me. It's time I returned home and faced up to what I did."

"They will kill you back home," Lenara said, her tone dismissive. "Not for what you did, but for who you are."

"You three have got to have better hearing than me." Mac turned to them. "Did any of you hear what they were talking about just now?"

"I'm afraid I wasn't listening," Teevar said, and Ral shrugged.

"She said something about blood," Mac said. "She's worried about someone, I know she is. We could use that somehow! We could say we know a good doctor and offer to take her there if she'll leave us alone—we can take her to Penvo. He was good, right?"

"I do not even know how to get back to Penvo," Lenara said.

Mac frowned. He sat himself by Teevar's side and stared at the door, determined to think of something.

MAC DIDN'T KNOW how much time had passed, but he was sure it must've been a couple of hours. Eventually the door opened again and Komeera, backed by two skreens, entered the room. The skreens moved forward to remove Lenara's cuffs.

"The three of you are free to leave. Teevar is now in my custody."

"Who's sick?" Mac asked, getting to his feet.

Komeera's cold gaze fell upon him. "Nobody."

"Somebody is. I heard you. You can play the cold-hearted cow all you like, but I saw that look on your face. You're worried about someone. We could help, you know."

The skreens left the room, and Komeera stepped back by the door. "I very much doubt that."

"We know of a doctor, very good, better than anybody you have. You let Teevar come with us and we'll tell you where to find him."

Komeera laughed. "Your desperation is almost charming, Mackenzie. I'm afraid Teevar will be staying with me. There is no doctor who can help us." She waved for them to leave.

Mac stayed stubbornly where he stood. "Us? Who's sick? What's wrong with them? Our doctor is a genius. I'm telling you. When Teevar was ill, he saved his life."

Komeera's gaze snapped to Teevar and she stepped into the room. "You were ill? How so?"

"Rotten blood." Teevar scowled at Komeera.

"The doctor saved you. How did he save you?"

"Mac saved me."

Mac looked from Teevar to Komeera. "It's a kovan, isn't it?" he said. "You've got a sick kovan on board. And he...she...they're bleeding? They don't have long left."

"You will help him," Komeera said.

Mac smiled and folded his arms. "Sod. Off."

Komeera stormed towards him and grabbed him by the front of his shirt. Lenara and Ral moved forwards, and Teevar cried out. Mac grinned.

"Sucks, doesn't it?" He took hold of Komeera's wrists and pushed her away. "I'll help you, but you let Teevar go. In fact, Teevar and Lenara leave now."

"Mac, no," Teevar said.

"Go now," Mac said again. "Ral can stay and hold my hand. You two go back to the ship and get the engines started. We're leaving as soon as I'm done here."

Teevar took hold of Mac's hand and turned him towards him. "You can't do this. You can't trust her. What you did for me took a lot out of you; you'll be at her mercy!"

"Ral will make sure I'm okay."

"If you can help," Komeera said, "truly help, then you have my word that I'll allow you to leave in peace. But if you are playing with me, I'll make you pay."

Mac nodded. Teevar looked back at him desperately as Lenara took hold of his shoulders and steered him to the door. "If you don't release him to me, I swear to the gods..." Teevar growled, glaring at Komeera, his eyes bright with tears. "I swear..."

Komeera looked at Mac once Lenara and Teevar had left. "Come with me."

Mac followed, Ral just behind him. "I'm not holding your hand," she said.

"Earth expression," Mac explained. "Don't worry. I won't make you hold my hand." He followed Komeera down a quiet corridor to a private, clean little room where a kovan male lay on a bed against the back wall. There was a woman attending him—Mac thought she was also kovan at first, until she turned when they entered and he saw her face. Her skin, blushed pink, had fine scales reminding him of a snake, and she had no nose—only two slits for nostrils.

"Nurse," Komeera said. "This man thinks he can help."

"I *can* help," Mac said, going to the bed. There was blood on the man's lips, and he was pale and still. "Are there other kovans on board? This disease is contagious."

"No. No other." Komeera joined Mac at the bedside and touched the man's face gently. "This is Melvar. My love. Please, whatever you can do, do it."

"He needs a blood transfusion." Mac rolled up his sleeve. "My blood. Nurse, can you...?"

The nurse nodded and pulled up a seat. She turned away to prepare for the transfusion. Mac sat and looked at Komeera. "I want Ral to stay here and watch over me," he said. "And I want you to bugger off."

"But—"

"Just go and wait outside. The nurse'll let you know when you can come back." He waited. Komeera hesitated, clearly torn between staying for Melvar and doing as Mac said. Eventually, she left the room.

Ral came and sat on the floor beside the bed. "If she changes her mind, I can't get us out of here. You saw what she did to me."

"Yeah. I just... I didn't want to be here on my own, and you're not worth anything to her. Sorry."

Ral showed him her teeth in a grin. "I thought you had a plan."

"Nope. I just hope Komeera keeps her word." He winced as the nurse slid the needle into his arm and then opened and closed his fist to get the blood flowing. He gazed at Melvar and then closed his eyes when he saw Teevar instead. He let out a deep sigh and settled back into the chair.

"Mac?"

Mac opened his eyes, saw a fuzzy face peering too close and closed them again. "Go 'way," he murmured.

"Mac, wake up for me. Please?"

Mac groaned and forced his eyes open again. Teevar was frowning at him. "What?"

"You're okay." Teevar leaned over and kissed Mac's forehead. "Ral carried you back. I thought you were dead at first, you were so pale."

Mac moved his gaze past Teevar and up at the ceiling, realising he was aboard the *Veena*. "Room's spinning. Where are we?"

"Heading away from the station. Komeera kept her word when her mate woke up and sent you back with Ral. They'd taken all our money, though, it's all gone."

Mac sighed. "Arseholes." *Lots of leafy veg,* he thought. *And a big juicy steak.* Teevar stroked his head, sending him back to sleep.

"I'll look after you now, Mac. You rest. I'll look after you."

Mac nodded and drifted away.

# Chapter Eighteen

IT TOOK MAC a couple of days before he began to feel relatively normal again. Teevar bought his meals to him, and he took advantage of the kovan's willingness to do stuff for him, lazing around in bed even when he could get up.

He popped a couple of berries in his mouth and watched Teevar massage his feet. "That feels good. You sure you don't mind?"

"I don't mind. You deserve it. We're free for a time. Nobody's chasing us."

"Mm." Mac flexed his toes and sucked juice from his fingers. "But some other bunch of bastards'll be after us soon, right? More bounty hunters."

"Yes," Teevar said quietly, concentrating on Mac's feet. "Or my people will come for me themselves."

Mac sat up, pulled his feet away from Teevar, and crawled down the end of the bed to him. "We'll go to Earth, the four of us, like we said."

Teevar touched Mac's face. "Lenara's taking us to where we first found you, but, my darling, don't get your hopes up. We still have to find this pin of yours."

Mac took Teevar's hand and kissed it. "The people I ran from will have it. I know they will. We'll go in there, all guns blazing. They'll have to give it back to me."

"I hope you're right."

Mac flopped back on the bed and scooped up another handful of berries. "I'm right. Relax." He patted the bed, and Teevar joined him. *Bloody hope I'm right.*

It took another four days—the days in space being the times between sleeps—to reach the place where Mac first arrived from Earth. As he stepped off the gangway and his shoes landed on the sandy ground, sending up little puffs, his heart stopped. It began again, thumping hard, as he gazed at the mishmash of buildings beyond the spacecrafts.

"Mac?" Teevar took his hand and gave it a squeeze. "Are you all right?"

"It's just...strange being back here, that's all."

"Do you remember where you arrived?" Lenara asked.

"I think so. Yeah." He nodded and set off towards the buildings. Lenara and Ral chatted behind him and Teevar stayed close by his side. He swallowed hard and stared at the buildings, at the streets, trying to remember which way to go. Silver spheres rolled past, and he stopped walking to gawk at them. The mark burned on his thigh.

"Mac?"

"I don't know," Mac said, staring. "I don't know where I arrived. I escaped—they were doing some shitty experiment on me—I ran and then I was arrested. I was taken in one of those things, but I passed out, I don't *remember* where...how..."

Teevar took Mac's face between his hands and gazed into his eyes. "We'll find it," he said. "Tell me what you remember."

"Kovans," Mac said. "It was kovans."

Teevar frowned. He kissed Mac and then turned to Ral and Lenara. "There are many different species here. Keep an eye out for any kovan-run businesses or areas. We'll speak to every damn kovan on the planet if we have to."

Mac smiled a little. "I think that's probably impossible, but thank you." Now that he was close, he wasn't sure he wanted to come face to face with the people who took him from Earth. Not after what they did to him. He walked along with the others anyway, making an attempt to look as if he was paying attention to his surroundings although in reality he was living in a daze.

Lenara grabbed him and Teevar suddenly and pulled them down a side street. He peered out to see what had spooked her and spotted a man wearing red and knew it was one of the law enforcement officers. Ral joined them a moment later, her tail flicking in apprehension.

"You three are known here?" she asked.

"Me and Lenara were arrested," Mac said. "Then we escaped. I guess they wouldn't hesitate to arrest us again. The bloke who took me in the first place seemed like an officious arsehole."

"Nobody knows me," Ral said. "Wait there."

She headed back out into the street before they could stop her. Mac groaned. "She's going to do something stupid." He touched his comms. "Ral, don't do anything stupid!"

He leaned back against the wall of the building and ran a hand through his hair. "Okay, let's think about this logically. They've only seen me naked or dressed in burlap; what are the chances they'll recognise me now?"

"They've seen you naked?" Teevar asked.

Mac waved a hand. "Long story."

He peered out into the street again and a man riding a rabbit-beast passed by. Mac shuddered. "Those rabbit things freak me out. Promise me if we're stealing anything this time it'll be something nonliving. I've ridden an ikk, that's enough of an experience for me." He ducked back into the shadows when he caught a flash of a red coat across the road. "What is Ral doing? Don't you think we should go and find her? If she gets herself caught again she's on her own."

"She seemed to have a plan," Teevar said. "I think the gods are on our side this time."

Mac suppressed a groan. He leaned back against the wall and looked at Lenara. She didn't seem as relaxed as Teevar, and he noticed how her hand rested on her gun. A silver sphere stopped at the end of the alley. Lenara drew her weapon—Mac, taking the hint, quickly drew his too and pointed it at the sphere.

A door opened and Ral looked out at them. "Get in. I've got us a ride."

Mac holstered his gun and hurried inside. There were only four chairs and a terrified-looking female kovan occupied one of them. He sat behind her and pulled Teevar onto his lap before he could protest as Lenara and Ral took the other two seats. The door closed and the seats rose into the air.

"The gods will repay you for your kindness," Teevar told the woman.

"I'm sure the gods know I didn't have much say in the matter," the woman replied as the sphere cleared to reveal the outside world. "I'm surprised at you, Pryster—sending your goon to threaten me."

Ral turned in her seat to look at them. "I asked nicely and she said no. I thought we were in a hurry."

Mac chuckled. "Good work. At least you didn't get arrested, eh?"

"Plenty of time for that," the woman muttered. She flicked her hand and the sphere spun into action, the buildings becoming blurs as they passed by.

"Does she know where she's going?" Mac asked, looking at Ral so he didn't have to look at anything else.

"She said there's a research centre run by kovans two blocks away."

The sphere stopped abruptly, and Mac's stomach lurched. He managed to keep hold of his lunch and let out a shaky breath as the chairs lowered to let them out. When the door opened and Teevar got up off his lap, he stared at the building before them. The last he'd seen of it had been when he'd glanced back over his shoulder as he'd run away.

The door snapped shut behind them and the sphere rolled away. Mac nodded. "This is the place."

"You tell us what you want to do, Mac," Lenara said.

*Run away.*

"I think you guys should pretend you're returning me. That'll get us inside. Then we find someone in charge—say you'll not release me over to them until they give you a reward—then pull a gun on the bastard and threaten them until they send us all to Earth."

"What if they're not that interested in you?" Ral asked.

"Come on," Mac scoffed. "Everybody's interested in me. I'm fascinating."

"It's too risky," Teevar said. "They could take you from us anyway. They could decide they want all of us. I think we should watch the place, wait until dark, and then break in. We'll find your pin ourselves."

"Okay," Mac agreed. "Yeah, that sounds better. Wait, what if that woman calls the rozzers on us?" He rolled his eyes when his companions stared blankly back at him. "The police. She could be fetching them right now."

"She won't." Ral flashed her teeth. "I told her I'd eat her children if she tried anything."

"Great." Mac wondered if lupas really did eat children. He shook his head, and turned his attention back to the building.

# Chapter Nineteen

NIGHT FELL OVER the city and the sky turned oddly orange, just as it did over Mac's city on Earth occasionally. There were no street lamps, but lights appeared nonetheless—strange floating orbs that drifted past just over their heads. The four of them had sat hidden in shadows across the street and watched as people left the building for the day—they looked like any other person leaving their place of work and not at all like the scary people dressed in white robes Mac had first encountered. They waited and waited longer still until nobody passed by anymore and the streets were quiet. Then they dashed out of their hiding place and ran up to the door, looking furtively over their shoulders in case anybody watched them.

"This isn't going to set off an alarm, is it?" Mac asked, pointing his gun at the door.

"Probably," Lenara said. "We'll deal with that once we're inside."

Mac fired at the door and kicked it open. Lenara turned as soon as they entered and shot up at something over the door—the alarm, Mac presumed. They closed the door behind them and stood in the half-light until their eyes adjusted.

"This place is creepy," Mac whispered.

"Smells too clean," Teevar said.

Lenara flicked a switch on her gun and a beam of light came out the end of it—for Mac's benefit, he supposed, though he was glad of it. The corridors were quiet and cold, and their footsteps echoed as they walked.

"Do you know where we should be looking?" Teevar asked.

"Not a clue." Mac stopped at a door, opened it a crack to peer inside, and then slipped into the room when he saw it was empty. It was an office of some sort, and Lenara shone the light for him as he rummaged through desk drawers.

"What does it look like?" Teevar asked, joining Mac in searching the room.

"Uh…" Mac frowned when he realised he couldn't remember exactly, though he was certain he'd recognise it when he saw it. "Silver and twisty. About…so big."

He looked up. Lenara stood by the door, shining the light, and Ral stood out in the corridor, keeping an eye out. "We might have to look all night," he said.

"Then we will," Teevar said. "Let's try the next room."

They left and walked down the corridor, peeling off to an open room on their right. Lenara's light bounced off a large glass jar, and Mac gasped. Lenara moved the light around the room, revealing rows of jars—each as big as they were—most containing some sort of pickled lifeform.

"Sick bastards." Mac peered in at a naked woman suspended in the green liquid. "I bet this is what they were going to do to me!"

Teevar clutched his pendant, a frown on his face, as he joined Mac beside the jar. He muttered a blessing and moved on to the next. Mac didn't have the heart to tell him they didn't have time. He wandered off on his own a little, but the bodies soon began to creep him out as he couldn't help but imagine eyes opening behind his back. He hurried back to the others with his skin crawling.

"We should try somewhere else," he suggested. "It's not here."

Suddenly, the lights came on and a voice sounded out from the other end of the room. The four of them scattered, and Mac crouched behind one of the jars, his heart racing. He peeked through the liquid and spotted two of the robed kovans wandering down the centre of the room.

"Honestly, you're hearing things," one of them said. "There's nobody here."

"I wish we could hurry up and wake these people up," the other replied. "I always feel like I'm being watched in here."

Mac shifted his gaze to the body in the jar he hid behind. The man hung lifeless and limp. *They're not dead?*

"Soon," the first kovan said. "It will be soon now. Come on."

Mac held his breath as the kovans turned and walked away. The lights turned off and he blinked into the dark until Lenara turned her torch on him once more.

"Do you want to leave?" she asked.

"No, we're so close." He did want to leave. He wanted to leave the whole damn planet and get back to Earth where it was only animals and onions people pickled. He headed out of the room quickly and chose another direction.

"I wonder how many more of them are here," he muttered to Teevar. "We need to be extra bloody careful."

They carried on, moving quickly, acutely aware of the noise of their footsteps on the hard floor. Mac tried another door only to find it locked, and deeming it worth the risk—for something important must be behind a locked door—he stepped back to let Lenara smash it open.

The room was white and empty but for a single chair in the middle of it. Mac's eyes widened. "This is it," he hissed. "This is the room they...they beamed me up into."

The four of them squeezed into the room, but Mac knew before they entered that the pin wasn't there. He cursed and kicked the chair over. Then, because he was so *fucking* angry all of a sudden, he picked the chair up and smashed it against the wall and kept smashing it until Teevar pulled him into a hug and held him close.

"It's okay," Teevar said. "It's okay."

Mac sobbed into his shoulder, fat, furious, frustrated tears which soaked into Teevar's clothes. He didn't even know why he was crying. He sniffed and pulled back to wipe his eyes. "I'm sorry. Get a fucking grip, Mac." He cleared his throat. "I'm all right. Just had a moment there; pretend that didn't happen."

"We'll keep looking," Teevar said, his voice gentle. He took Mac's hand and led him from the room.

And straight into two *armed* kovans. Mac, acting on instinct, drew his weapon and fired. Teevar cried out. The kovans fired back and pain ripped through Mac's stomach as if he'd been punched in the gut. He fell, not quite sure what had happened, Teevar catching him before he hit the ground. People were shouting. Lenara had her hands in the air, her gun hanging loose in her grip. Ral bared her teeth.

Mac touched his stomach and then lifted his hands to touch Teevar's face. He frowned when he left a bloodied mark on the kovan's cheek. "You're bleeding," he muttered.

"No," Teevar said, his eyes bright with tears as he cradled Mac's head in his lap. "No, no, no. Stay with me, Mac. Stay with me."

Without his pin, Mac wasn't going anywhere. He smiled and everything went dark.

*MARTIN MAY HAVE been fat, but he had an attractive face and a nice house and a generous nature Mac fully intended to take advantage of. Mac stood naked in the doorway of the bedroom, a glass of orange juice in his hand, watching the other man sleep. Eventually, a cool breeze around his backside made him close the door and slip into bed beside Martin. He leaned over to put the glass on the bedside table.*

*"Ethan?"*

*"Go back to sleep," Mac said.*

*"Ethan, would you like a new watch?" Martin murmured. "I'll buy you a new watch. You're so good to me. Stay with me tonight won't you, darling? Don't slip away before dawn. Stay with me."*

*"Mm," Mac said. "I'm not going anywhere."*

MAC WOKE WITH a sharp intake of breath and his heart fluttering unpleasantly. Images flashed through his mind of people suspended inside glass jars, of *himself* breathing in green liquid, of being trapped while Teevar watched on.

"Teevar?"

Everything was so white he could barely see properly. He had a moment of panic, thinking he'd gone blind, but then somebody gripped his hand tight and Teevar appeared over him with a worried frown on his face.

"You're awake! Thank the gods."

"I'm still here?"

"We thought we'd lost you. You've been out for days—Kansha had to put you into suspension to keep you alive. I honestly thought I'd lost you. Mac..."

"Slow down." Mac lifted a hand to rub his eyes. "What happened? Where am I?" He forced himself up a little, and Teevar fussed around him, propping another pillow under his head. Mac could see he was in some sort of hospital room, and he was alone but for Teevar. "Where are the girls?"

"They're fine. They're around somewhere. They'll be in to visit you soon."

"Those fuckers shot me." Mac touched his stomach. "Where am I?"

"At the research centre," Teevar said. "But, Mac, they're not bad people. They're scientists. And you, you're amazing; you're so special—"

Mac laughed because he didn't quite know what Teevar was on about. "We need to get out of here. Get the girls. They're *bad* people—they shot me in the guts and they keep people in jars—not to mention the shit they did to me when I first arrived. They marked me. My thigh. We're out of here. Help me up." He struggled to sit up and swung his legs out of the bed.

"Mac, please rest. You'll hurt yourself!"

Mac ignored him. His bare feet had just touched the cold floor when a woman entered the room and hurried to his bedside.

"You shouldn't be up," she said, pressing him back down. "Teevar, you're supposed to be watching him. You should've come and got me the moment he woke up."

"You can't keep me here." Mac scowled as he lay back down.

"No, I can't," she agreed, "But please rest. Your body is still recovering from huge trauma."

"Yeah, your people shot me."

She bristled. "I believe you shot first."

"Didn't hit anyone, though," Mac muttered.

Teevar raised his hands. "It's all right, Kansha. I'll make sure he rests. Thank you."

Kansha pursed her lips. She gave a brusque nod and left the room once more. Teevar returned to Mac's bedside and took hold of his hand.

"She's a doctor," he explained. "She saved your life."

Mac's head was spinning now and his limbs were heavy. He heaved a sigh. "Why do you trust them? You can't trust someone just because they're the same species as you, you know. I know plenty of humans who'd happily screw me over as soon as look at me."

Teevar reached over and brushed Mac's hair away from his forehead. "They're working towards a cure for Ferotte's disease—the rotten blood. The people we saw in the jars, they're not dead; they're in suspension. As soon as there's a cure, they'll be able to live again." He lifted Mac's hand to his lips and kissed it. "You're the one who'll save us all."

Mac didn't like the sound of that. He had visions of the kovans draining his blood until he was nothing but a dry, old husk. He swallowed and eyed the machinery he was hooked up to, wondering if he could free himself and get out of there without anybody noticing.

"I want to go," he muttered.

"When you're better, Mac. They always meant to send you home. Kansha tells me you ran before they could send you back."

"I was *frightened*." Mac glared at Teevar. Why didn't he understand? Why wasn't he on Mac's side? His head was fuzzy. Had they drugged him? "Of course I bloody ran! Do you know what they did to me? They took me from my home and they assaulted me and explained *nothing*, and I was so fucking freaked out!"

Concern was written all over Teevar's face, but Mac ignored it. He pulled his hand free and rolled onto his side, away from the kovan.

"Mac, I need to tell you something. Kansha said she'd explain, but I think it'd be better if it came from me. Mac?"

Mac sniffed and stared at the wall opposite. If they could send him home, they should damn well send him home, not keep him there cooped up.

"Mac, what they did to you...they took a cell sample."

"Cell sample, my arse. Why didn't they just scrape my fucking cheek?"

"They used your sample to...to make new life, to impregnate some of the women. The hope is that with your genes, the next generation will be immune to the disease. They'll work with the youngsters to create a cure. You'll be saving millions of lives."

*I'm gonna be a daddy.* Mac closed his eyes as a warm tear ran down his cheek. "I didn't want any of this. They shouldn't have just taken from me. Maybe if they'd have *asked*..."

Teevar rested his hand on Mac's shoulder but Mac shrugged him away. "They went about it all wrong," he agreed softly. "I was angry too when they told me. They treated you as an alien test subject and not as the sentient, *wonderful* human being you are. They were *wrong*, and I wish I'd been there when you'd first arrived, to hold you when you were scared."

"You didn't know me. You wouldn't have cared." Mac shifted himself onto his back and looked at Teevar again. "I'm tired. Can you go, please? I just want to sleep."

"Of course." Teevar got to his feet, leaned over to kiss Mac on the forehead and then left the room.

Mac stared at the ceiling for a long time after he'd left. Eventually he rolled down the bedcovers to inspect his stomach—he had a small round scar just below the ribs on his right-hand side. He was wearing his own trousers, he noticed, but he was topless and frowned over the loss of one of his favourite shirts.

*I'm gonna be a daddy.*

He was nothing more than a sperm donor. He'd be famous though, surely. The saviour of an alien race and the father of a new one. Half-human, half-kovan hybrids. The thought pleased him more than it probably should've done and he scowled and folded his arms across his chest.

*Narcissistic bastard*, he told himself.

He stared into space once more, until he couldn't keep his eyes open.


RAL AND LENARA visited him, and Teevar sat by his side most of the time. Kansha came and removed the needles from his arms and helped him to walk. She answered any question he asked her and assured him that yes, they could send him back to Earth.

"Only you, though," she said. "The pin is attuned to your biological signature and simply wouldn't work for your friends. When we send you back, you'll be going alone."

That caused an ache in his chest he couldn't quite shift. Mac didn't mention anything to his friends about it. He was sure they already knew. He hadn't made his mind up whether he'd go or not. He loved Teevar, but he belonged on Earth, didn't he? Hadn't all the crap that had happened to him proved that? Besides, Teevar had already begun to distance himself—watching from the doorway or hardly speaking. Mac figured that was a good thing.

Still, though, he didn't want to leave things like that. It was dark in the room and he was alone. He pushed off the bed covers and got up, reaching for the clothes somebody had left for him on the chair beside the bed. He dressed and then padded barefoot from the room and out into the corridor. He had no idea where Teevar was.

A scuff behind him made him turn and he almost jumped out of his skin when Lenara loomed up out of the shadows. "What the bloody hell?"

"I did not mean to startle you."

"What are you lurking about in the dark for?"

"I was waiting for you."

"In the dark?" Mac shook his head. "I'll never understand you people. What did you want?"

"You should know something, about Teevar."

Mac sighed. Was this something he was going to want to know? He waited for Lenara to speak. She glanced back over her shoulder and then stepped closer to him. "I had to wait until he wasn't around because he wouldn't tell you himself, but I think you deserve to know."

"Know what, Lenara?"

"Teevar's being detained by the kovans. They lock him in at night. He has agreed to hand himself in to the authorities back on his planet if the people here send you home."

Mac closed his eyes briefly. He reached out a hand to steady himself against the wall as the ache in his chest intensified. "He's what? But they'll send me home anyway, right? They never meant for me to stay."

"They saw an opportunity and they took it. If Teevar runs, they'll not help you."

"Bastards." Mac stared at the wall as if he'd find instruction written there. He let out a slow breath and straightened up, knowing there really was only one thing he could do. "Right, where is he?"

Lenara smiled. "Come with me."

Mac followed Lenara down the corridor, aware she was doing something she shouldn't have been, judging by the furtive looks she gave as she peered around corners and checked through cracks in doors before proceeding. He noticed a figure in the gloom ahead, waiting outside a door, and relaxed when he recognised it was only Ral. The lupa got to her feet.

"You told him?" she asked.

"She told me," Mac confirmed. He looked at the door and then tried the handle, though he knew it'd be locked. "Lenara, could you...?"

He stepped back as Lenara lowered her head and rammed her horns into the door. The wood cracked and split, and it took another hit before it opened up. Teevar got to his feet as Mac entered the room.

"What are you doing? You can't be in here!"

"Come to get you out," Mac said. "Come on."

"No." Teevar sat back down on the bed and clutched his pendant in his hand. "I have to do this. If I don't hand myself in, they won't send you home. I can't deny you that."

Mac sat on the bed beside Teevar. "I'm not letting you hand yourself in. You've got to keep running."

"Absolutely not."

Mac took Teevar's hand away from his pendant and held it in his. "Run with me."

"No!" Teevar turned to Mac and clutched both his hands tight. "This is your chance to go home, back to Earth! You have to go home!"

Mac shrugged. "Why would I want to go there without you, eh?" He glanced at Ral and Lenara keeping guard at the door. There was only one thing that mattered now. "I love you, you daft sod. We'll find Earth another way. Come on."

He got to his feet, hoping to pull Teevar with him, but Teevar stayed stubbornly seated. "You don't know what you're talking about. It must be the painkillers."

"I'm not taking any painkillers." Mac pulled Teevar to his feet and kissed him before he could protest, feeling the warmth and passion in the other man's lips as he gave in to him. The world seemed to spin around him and then condense to that one moment—to the two of them.

Teevar pulled back, his eyes wide. "I love you too," he said.

Mac grinned. "Good. Ready to run?"

Teevar nodded and the two of them headed to the door together. "Better run fast," Lenara said. "I can hear them coming."

They ran out into the corridor then, and just as Lenara said, urgent footsteps echoed around them, and then shouts and they saw the first white-robed kovan around the corner.

"You can take your pin," Mac yelled at them, "and you can shove it up your arse!"

He took Teevar's hand and ran, wondering where the hell his shoes were as he went.

# About the Author

Emma Jane has been writing stories since primary school, some of which still survive in notebooks in her dad's attic, and wanted to be an author as soon as she realised it was a possible career choice and 'Pony' or 'Ninja' weren't viable options.

Her first short story, Club Freak, about an anonymous woman's determination to find her husband's killer, was published by Park Publication's Debut magazine in May 2009. Since then, she has gone on to write many short stories and poems for various small presses and has achieved an Honourable Mention in the 2011 Writers of the Future competition.

In 2014, writing as Emma Jane, she signed her first publishing contract for not one, but two novels. *Otherworld* formerly published by Torquere Press, and *Shuttered* by Dreamspinner Press.

Email: em_jane_82@yahoo.co.uk

Twitter: @emizzy

Website: www.ejtett.weebly.com

# Also by

Whitecott Manor

# Also Available from NineStar Press

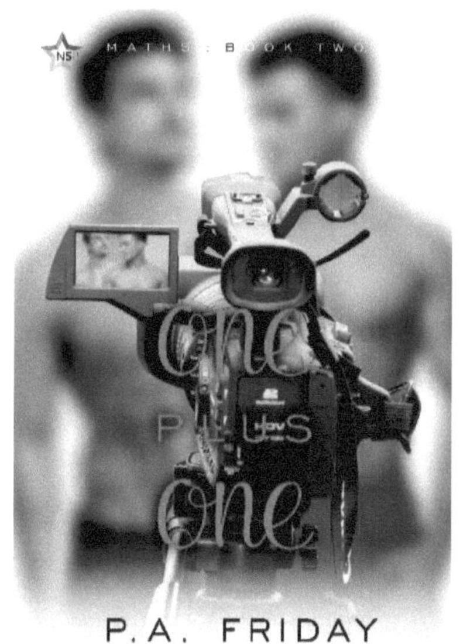

# Connect with NineStar Press

www.ninestarpress.com

www.facebook.com/ninestarpress

www.facebook.com/groups/NineStarNiche

www.twitter.com/ninestarpress

www.tumblr.com/blog/ninestarpress

www.ingramcontent.com/pod-product-compliance
Lightning Source LLC
Chambersburg PA
CBHW051704180726
48283CB00004B/1205